Samuel French Acting Edition

I0591856

The Butter and Egg Man

by George S. Kaufman

SAMUELFRENCH.COM   SAMUELFRENCH.CO.UK

FOR PRODUCTION ENQUIRIES

UNITED STATES AND CANADA

Info@SamuelFrench.com

1-866-598-8449

UNITED KINGDOM AND EUROPE

Plays@SamuelFrench.co.uk

020-7255-4302

Each title is subject to availability from Samuel French, depending upon country of performance. Please be aware that *THE BUTTER AND EGG MAN* may not be licensed by Samuel French in your territory. Professional and amateur producers should contact the nearest Samuel French office or licensing partner to verify availability.

For all enquiries regarding motion picture, television, and other media rights, please contact Samuel French.

MUSIC USE NOTE

Licensees are solely responsible for obtaining formal written permission from copyright owners to use copyrighted music in the performance of this play and are strongly cautioned to do so. If no such permission is obtained by the licensee, then the licensee must use only original music that the licensee owns and controls. Licensees are solely responsible and liable for all music clearances and shall indemnify the copyright owners of the play(s) and their licensing agent, Samuel French, against any costs, expenses, losses and liabilities arising from the use of music by licensees. Please contact the appropriate music licensing authority in your territory for the rights to any incidental music.

IMPORTANT BILLING AND CREDIT REQUIREMENTS

If you have obtained performance rights to this title, please refer to your licensing agreement for important billing and credit requirements.

Copy of the original program of "The Butter and
Egg Man" Produced by Crosby Gaige at the Long-
acre Theatre, New York, September 23, 1925, with
the following cast:

PETER JONES .... *Gregory Kelly*
JANE WESTON .... *Sylvia Field*
JOE LEHMAN .... *Robert Middlemass*
FANNY LEHMAN .... *Lucille Webster*
JACK McCLURE .... *John A Butler*
MARY MARTIN .... *Marion Barney*
A WAITER .... *Tom Fadden*
CECIL BENHAM .... *. Harry Neville*
BERNIE SAMPSON .... *Harry Stubbs*
PEGGY MARLOWE .... *. Eloise Stream*
KITTY HUMPHREYS .... *Puritan Townsend*
OSCAR FRITCHIE .... *Denman Maley*
A. J. PATTERSON .... *. George Alison*

Staged by James Gleason.

SYNOPSIS OF SCENES

ACT I: *Office of Lehmac Productions, Inc., New
York City.*

ACT II: *A Hotel Room in Syracuse.*
SCENE I: *Just before the Opening.*
SCENE II: *Just after the Opening.*

ACT III: *The Office A few weeks later.*

DESCRIPTION OF CHARACTERS

JOE LEHMAN *is about forty. Except for a colored shirt, his clothes are not of the kind known as loud, and yet he has the knack of making them seem a bit exaggerated. He bulks large and forceful as he sits in his desk chair—cigar in mouth, derby hat on head, one clenched fist thoughtfully pounding an open palm* JOE LEHMAN *gets his effects by solid driving*

JACK McCLURE *is a more ingratiating type.* MAC, *as a matter of fact, is even rather attractive. About thirty-five. His attire is up to the minute and a shade beyond it; he wears a fashionable gray soft hat.*

FANNY LEHMAN *is a woman in the late thirties, perhaps, with an enormous poise and an insolent assurance acquired in years of touring the South Bends and the Wichitas*

JANE WESTON *is twenty or so, and, since she is the heroine of this fable, she is good-looking and neatly dressed. She is* LEHMAN'S *stenographer and office girl.*

MARY MARTIN *is the familiar type of slightly passée actress.*

PETER JONES *is a boy of twenty-one or so, and it may be said without exaggeration that there are some things he does not know about the world For the rest, he is simple, likable, and just about average.*

CECIL BENHAM *is a calm, reserved and dignified Englishman, who is even able to wear a monocle without suggesting musical comedy*

5

BERNIE SAMPSON *is a slightly Semitic young man with that air of sophistication about him that can be acquired only through long service on Broadway.*

PEGGY MARLOWE *is a smartly dressed and ever so good-looking chorus girl*

KITTY HUMPHREYS, *a pretty switchboard girl*

OSCAR FRITCHIE *is a sufficiently nice-looking young man, but just a little dumb.*

PATTERSON *is a middle-aged business man, rather formidable in manner.*

ACT I

SCENE: *The office of Lehmac Productions, Inc. It is situated in any one of the buildings that sprinkle Broadway above Forty-second Street.*

The Lehmac office has been only lately taken possession of. A pile of miscellaneous junk from an old office occupies a large part of the rear wall. There are great bundles of newspapers, most of them copies of Christmas issues of "The Morning Telegraph," containing MR LEHMAN'S advertised seasonal greetings to all artists everywhere, there are a few mouldy box files, part of a stray, bespangled costume, and even a ballet dancer's slipper. Except for a huge and shining and obviously new desk, the pile is the most prominent object in the room

The other furniture is likewise new; a swivel chair at the desk left center, a visitors' chair in front of it, a smaller chair left. There is a filing cabinet right of center door, but from the outside it looks as if there were nothing in it. A water-cooler left of center door. Some sixty or seventy photographs of artists are on the walls in interesting disarray They are all inscribed.

7

"With love to Joe," "To Joe from La Belle Mar-
guery," "To the Greatest Agent in the World"
—inscriptions, plainly, that bespeak a business
affiliation rather than a personal bond.

There are two doors; one to a small office at
the Right, the other directly to the outer hall-
way. The door at the Right is unlettered; when
it is opened one catches a glimpse of the recep-
tion room without. The other door is exactly
center, and is lettered as follows on the reverse
side of its frosted glass:

ROOM 806

LEHMAC PRODUCTIONS,
INC.

Entrance Room 805

Across the hall, when the center door is
opened, is another office door; a door announc-
ing that it is the office of "Stein, Birchfelder &
Blaumann, Attorneys-at-Law," and setting
forth, in a corner below, the additional names of
"Leo Heymann" and "A. J. Carmody."

The rising curtain reveals MR LEHMAN *and*
his confrère, JACK McCLURE, *deeply and none*
too amiably in thought JOE LEHMAN *is about*
forty. Except for a colored shirt, his clothes
are not of the kind known as loud, and yet he
has the knack of making them seem a bit exag-
gerated He bulks large and forceful as he sits
in his desk chair—cigar in mouth, derby hat on
head, one clenched fist thoughtfully pounding

an open palm. JOE LEHMAN gets his effects by solid driving. JACK McCLURE is a more ingratiating type. MAC, as a matter of fact, is even rather attractive. About thiry-five. His attire is up to the minute and a shade beyond it; he wears a fashionable gray soft hat The hats of LEHMAN and McCLURE remain on their heads throughout the three acts, they are a part of them, and you could hardly imagine them bareheaded.

MAC *discovered in chair* R *of desk, lighting cigarette, straw hat on back of head.* LEHMAN *discovered sitting* L. *of desk, feet up, cigar in mouth, derby over eyes.*

LEHMAN. *(Pauses, rises, crosses up* L *; gets idea, snaps fingers, crosses to 'phone on upper end of desk, takes off receiver and jiggles receiver piece)* Get me Sol David *(Hangs up)* He come through for that Jenny show last year.

MAC Never got a nickel back. *(Tosses burnt match to ashtray on desk)* I saw the statements.

LEHMAN. *(Crosses down* L.*)* Anybody comes in on this trick'll clean up. I can do it for fifteen thousand I'd take twelve.

MAC. You'd take one

LEHMAN. *(Crosses to* L. *of desk)* You don't say? Let me tell you this, Sweetheart—there ain't going to be no bargains, not if I have to throw—*('Phone rings)*—it in the ashcan. *(Picks up 'phone, takes off receiver and holds mouthpiece against chest as he still talks to* MAC*)* This show's a pipe, and any bird that comes in is going to make plenty *(Speaks in 'phone)* Hello! Right! Is Sol David there?— This is Joe Lehman talking. Oh—no. *(Hangs up)* Bermuda Beats hell how far away they can get when you're trying to raise coin *(Crosses down L)*

MAC   Here's a slant! Remember them income lists the papers published—taxes?

LEHMAN. We ain't got no time to—*(Crosses up around desk to C)*—follow them up. I got to get a bankroll before morning or I can't rehearse no longer. *(Turns to MAC as he reaches C.)* Huh! That's Equity for you !

MAC. Tough luck they had to grab Ackerman just when they did

LEHMAN   I woulda had his check this morning. *(Starts up around desk again to L)* Then he has to go and get pinched with them four cases in the car—— I don't link up with no more bootleggers *(Crosses down L and hold)*

MAC   *(Thoughtfully)* There's a fellow makes lithographs   He sunk some coin in a two-for-one last year—Everson

LEHMAN   A bowl of cherries   When you going to meet this other bird?

MAC. Lots of time—it's right downstairs. Anyway, he wants a musical—you know—girl stuff

LEHMAN   Ten thousand, I could do this trick of mine for *(Looking front)*

MAC   Say—there was two fellows named Levi, in ladies' shirtwaists——

LEHMAN. They got bit *(Crosses up to L. end of desk)* When I think the way—*(Leans over upper end of desk)*—them ham managers can go out and get bank accounts for bum shows—and here I got the best proposition in twenty years

MAC   *(Still seated)* You know what that downtown bunch got set back for half of Sid Ehrman's show ? I got the inside on it—ninety grand.

LEHMAN   *(Crosses away to L)* You'd think they'd get wise after awhile, with them shows they put on   Ain't nothing but luck puts half of 'em over   That one of Ziegfeld's the other night. *(Crosses back to L. of desk, leans over on C.)* You seen it

MAC. A turkey.

LEHMAN Junk scenery—— *(Crosses L.).* Bunch of costumes I wouldn't send over the Pan time. But he gets away with it. Dumb luck! *(Cigar in mouth, looking front)*

MAC The public'll get on to him some day.

LEHMAN Comedy bits they kicked off the— *(Leaning over C. of desk)*—Columbia Wheel ten years ago. And here I am with a compact little drama, up to the minute, and I can't grab even eight, ten thousand to get the curtain up. *(Sits L of desk.)*

MAC *(Leans over in chair)* Listen, Joe—on the level, can't you get it out of Fanny? *(Turns to L on chair.)*

LEHMAN. Do I look like a sap? Ain't I told you me and her was up to six o'clock this morning, jawing about it? There ought to be some law against a wife having a lot of property in her own name. *(Looks front L., elbow on arm of chair, cheek resting on palm of hand)*

MAC But look what you done for her   You took her out of that five-a-day and put her on Broadway   Didn't you tell her that?

LEHMAN I didn't tell her nothing else for four hours   And she ain't only got the shack in Freeport —she's got a hunk in the bank come due on a bond or something, and she's going to buy another slice of Long Island with it   Beats all how them vaudeville hams ain't happy unless they're buying up a bunch of bum lots *(Feet on table.)*

MAC. *(Rises, crosses up to door)* Well—it's about time for me to slide down

LEHMAN. Don't bring nobody up here without you ring me *(FANNY knocks once off C.)* Open up —it's Fanny

(MAC *throws open the door.* FANNY LEHMAN
*stands without—a woman in the late thirties,
perhaps, with an enormous poise and an insolent assurance acquired in years of touring the
South Bends and the Wichitas. She does not
even give* MAC *a contemptuous glance. Instead,
her eyes go to* LEHMAN, *who is leaning far back
in his swivel chair, his feet on the desk.* FANNY
*drifts down to the desk and plants herself
squarely in* LEHMAN'S *line of vision She has
fortified herself with evidence with which to
continue the battle begun at home, and she feels
pleasantly sure of herself. There is a world of
insolence in her opening speech)*

LEHMAN. Well? (MAC *stays up* C *by filing cabinet.)*

FANNY. I just been taking a peep at that trick
troupe of yours

LEHMAN. Yeh? Well, you keep out of them rehearsals, you hear me? *(Rises, crosses down* L *)*

FANNY. You got a show there that's going to
make history, do you know it? They're going to
date things from the time you—*(Leaning against
lower* R. *end of desk)*—open this one.

LEHMAN *(Looking at her)* I ain't asked you
what you think about it

FANNY. *(Still leaning on* R *end of desk)* I caught
that bit where the leading lady was supposed to be
sixteen or something and climbing up apple trees
The thing to make them trees out of is reinforced
concrete.

LEHMAN. All right It ain't your money, is it?

FANNY. No. You bet it ain't, dearie. *(Puts purse
on table; crosses in front below desk)* And I gather
that so far it ain't nobody else's (LEHMAN *crosses
to water-bottle up* L C *)*

MAC. Now, listen—*(Crosses down to her, below desk L C.)*—Fanny—Joe's in a hole.

FANNY Well, if it ain't Close-mouth!

MAC *(To FANNY at L C)* I only want to help you both. Now, Joe's got a nice little entertainment —that's all it is, a good entertainment—— *(JOE, at water-bottle up L C, fills glass)* Ain't it, Joe? And he can ring up on it for ten thousand. Now, you're his own wife and he's your husband, and you got all this property——

FANNY Save your voice for the sucker. *(MAC starts R.)*

LEHMAN *(At water-bottle)* Let her alone *(Up L.C Crosses to C)* She don't care nothing about me. That's women. *(MAC up R C.)* You wouldn't 'a' had a sou if I hadn't dug you out of that Texas honky-tonk and steered you onto Broadway. I put you in regular vaudeville, that's what I done for you.

FANNY *(Leaning on front of desk)* Well—you got yours, didn't you? All the acts is on to agents like you. Twenty-per-cent Joe.

LEHMAN Fanita, the world's greatest juggler! Hah! If it wasn't for me you'd be keeping four clubs in the air right now for some Gus Sun that nobody ever heard of.

FANNY *(Crosses R to JOE)* Don't you four-club me! I done six clubs for the wow at the finish, and done it for years.

LEHMAN Aaah! There ain't a stage between here and California ain't got dents in it from them clubs of yours. *(FANNY crosses to lower end of desk. MAC gets up in front of filing cabinet)* They wouldn't let nobody sit in the first five rows. *(She gives LEHMAN a look. LEHMAN crosses up and back)* Fanita!

FANNY. Yes, Fanita. And I'm as good today as I ever was.

LEHMAN   Just about. *(Crosses R., hands behind back, cigar in mouth.)*

FANNY. All right, all right I was a bum juggler and you were a great agent. But—I got the house and lot in Freeport and you're trying to get it. *(She looks front LEHMAN gives her a look and as MAC speaks turns his back to foots)*

MAC. *(Takes couple of steps down to her)* What are you going to do with your money, Fanny—leave it to a home for jugglers?

FANNY. Say, listen, don't you go worrying none about the jugglers They can take care of themselves. *(Hold at desk)* They ain't none of—*(Takes a couple of steps up, back to footlights)*—them hanging on to the edge of show business, pretending to know all about it just because they bum a lunch at the Astor every day *(Angrily)* And what are you doing in here, anyhow? Me and Joe can get along without you.

MAC. *(At door C)* I'll go down and meet that certain party *(Exits C)*

LEHMAN. *(Crosses up around desk FANNY watches him. As she places hand on hip, he takes a startled step away, still crossing L.)* Why don't you go home if—— *(Sits)* you're so crazy about it? *(Cigar in mouth)*

FANNY Now, listen—— *(Crosses to R of desk)* Joe—this ain't your game Why don't you go back to agenting, where you know the ropes?

LEHMAN. Because I don't want to,— *(Slaps table)* see? I'm in the legit from now on

FANNY All right But you ain't going to get anyone to sink any money in that junk show—I seen a rehearsal *(Sits R of desk)*

LEHMAN I don't want no advice *(Rises)* Go on home *(Crosses down L)*

FANNY All right, go on and produce it Produce it with some butter-and-egg man's coin and that dame of the Colonial Revolution that you got in the leading role.

LEHMAN. *(Crosses below desk to R)* Never you mind about Martin. She's going to make the hit of her life *(Looks front, cigar in mouth)*

FANNY. I ain't got nothing against her. I suppose she either had to join up with your troupe or go back to her original role in "The Two Orphans" (LEHMAN *gives her a look.)* Who tipped you off to her, the British Museum?

LEHMAN. Just because— *(Crosses back of desk)* you ain't never heard of her, don't say she ain't good *(Crosses to windows L. and looks out, smoking.)*

FANNY Say—my not hearing of her don't prove nothing. They didn't have no rotogravure sections in them days What's her name again?

LEHMAN. Her name is Mary Martin and it'll— *(Sits, looks front, cigar in mouth)* be up in lights

FANNY Mary Martin. And what a temper she's got! Why, I wasn't even talking to her.

LEHMAN. *(Turns and looks at her, takes ashtray and carefully places it on L of desk)* You mean you let fly one of them wisecracks at that rehearsal?

FANNY I never opened my mouth.

LEHMAN. What did you say?

FANNY I merely asked a question

LEHMAN. What was it—when was she born?

FANNY. I told you I caught her in that scene where she's mama's little darling—playing around cherry trees.

LEHMAN Well—and what was your question?

FANNY I says to the Director—"What does she wear in that scene?"

LEHMAN. Go on.

FANNY And he says—"blue pants."

LEHMAN *Then* comes the gag.

FANNY. I just says—"Drop your curtain on that laugh." *(Rises, crosses up* R.C *)*

LEHMAN. *(Crosses above desk to* FANNY R.C.*)* Oh, you did, did you? And if Martin goes and has hysterics on me, I suppose that don't mean nothing to you, does it?—But what about me? I suppose you're trying to see how much you can help, when here I am sweating blood trying to get this show on and worried all the time about——— *(Cries and crosses away to* L *)*

(JANE WESTON enters somewhat uncertainly from the reception room. She is twenty or so, and, since she is the heroine of this fable, she is good-looking and neatly dressed. She is LEHMAN'S stenographer and office girl She closes the door and stands)

LEHMAN. I'd think the least a——— *(Crosses back to* FANNY*)* man's wife could do——— What is it?

JANE *(At door)* Miss Martin is outside

FANNY. Wheel her in

LEHMAN. *(Looks at* FANNY*)* Take them small time jokes and get out of here *(Starts* L *; stops at* C *)* Is she behaving all right? *(Crosses* L *to desk at upper end)*

JANE Why—yes, sir.

LEHMAN. Not crying or nothing?

JANE. No, sir

FANNY Has she got a knife?

LEHMAN *(Above desk* L.C. *and hold)* You get out! Bring her in! Go on, I don't want no scenes in here! *(JANE opens door* R *)*

FANNY. *(Indicating distance from door to desk)* I want to see if she can make it to the desk.

JANE *(Enters, holds door open for* MARTIN*)* Miss Martin.

(MARY MARTIN *enters* R. *She is the familiar type of slightly passée actress She stops short as she sees* FANNY; *draws herself up.*)

FANNY. *(Up to* C. *door)* Can you imagine? Blue pants. *(Exits up* C. JANE *exits* R)

(READY 'Phone.)

MARTIN. *(After* FANNY *and* JANE *exit)* Well—

LEHMAN. *(Crosses to back desk)* Don't pay no attention to her. *(Sits)* She's loco. What's on— *(Looks at papers)* your mind?

MARTIN. *(Crosses to desk)* It's a check of yours, Mr. Lehman. It just came back to me for the third time (LEHMAN *looks at check)* What does that entitle me to—permanent possession?

LEHMAN. *(Looking over check)* Wait a while and put it through again *(Hands her back check.)*

MARTIN. I want the money. I need it.

LEHMAN. *(Looking through papers)* All right— you're going to get it. You just got to wait. That's all

MARTIN Mr Lehman, I think a shoestring would be big for what you're operating on. And unless I get fifty right now—— *(Raps on desk with right hand)* I'm going straight to Equity and tell the whole story They'll call out the company. *(Turns back on* LEHMAN JANE *starts typing off* R. *and keeps it up until* LEHMAN *opens door.)*

LEHMAN *(Rises and leans on desk)* Now listen, Sweetheart You got a great part in a great show and you're going to be great in it *(Pats her on left shoulder)* We're all going to make a pile of coin, and if you just string along with us——

MARTIN. *(Angry)* That's what you said the last time This time I want the money

LEHMAN Well, you don't get it, see? Not till I'm good and ready *(Sits)* A lot of real stars would give their eye teeth to play the part you got. *('Phone rings)*

('PHONE.)

MARTIN. Well, if that's the way you feel about it—— *(Crosses R.C.)*

LEHMAN *(At 'phone impatiently)* Yes? Mac? What is it? She's gone. What is it—a live one? Bring him up Where are you, downstairs? Right! Hey, keep a hold of his arm. *(Hangs up)* Now clear out. *(Rises, crosses to MARTIN)* I got business.

MARTIN. *(Crosses to LEHMAN)* And the money?

LEHMAN. Listen! You'll get your money. We're taking in a partner, a millionaire See? *(Starts R)* Miss Weston——

MARTIN. *When* do I get it?

LEHMAN. *(Crosses down R. to door)* Come back in half an hour you can have all the money you want. I tell you he's a big millionaire Miss Weston! *(Opens door R)*

JANE. *(Discovered typing, enters R.)* Yes, sir?

LEHMAN. *(To JANE)* Now, get this—— *(Then to MARTIN)* Will you get the hell out of here?

MARTIN. I'll give you just half an hour. Then I'm coming back. *(Exits up C.)*

LEHMAN. *(Crosses L to desk)* Clean this place up There's a big butter-and-egg man coming.

JANE Yes, sir. *(Shuts door R. and crosses to up R.C)*

LEHMAN. And shake a leg. *(Clears desk, putting papers in drawers.)*

JANE Yes, sir. *(Crosses up C. Picks up papers from floor)* Who did you say was coming, Mr Lehman?

LEHMAN. *(Busy at desk)* A butter-and-egg man. Don't you know what a butter-and-egg man is? A millionaire! A millionaire! He's going to put money in the show.

JANE   Oh, I'm glad of that   *(Picking up papers and puts them in drawer of filing cabinet.)*

LEHMAN.   I thought you'd get it after a while *(Sits, looks in cigar box in drawer on up stage end, and shuts drawer)*

JANE   *(Crosses down to R of desk, she has three or four sheets of typed paper)* Yes, sir   *(Slight pause)* Does that mean you'll pay me my salary then?

LEHMAN.   *(Stops, takes cigar out of mouth)* You're going to begin, too, huh?

JANE.   I've been here four weeks

LEHMAN.   *(Closes drawer, which he has left open on down stage end)* All right   You'll get it

JANE.   Thanks   *(Crosses up to filing cabinet again)*

LEHMAN   *(Gets idea as he closes drawer, crosses to JANE at L of filing cabinet)* And look here— when this guy's been in here a while, you make an entrance with a piece of paper, see? A letter, any-thing—make it busy   Put it on my desk

JANE   Yes, sir   *(Holds position up R.C)*

LEHMAN   Don't stop to take no bows—just exit *(Starts back to desk)*

JANE   Yes, sir   (MAC *enters* R, *closes door and crosses to* C)

LEHMAN   *(Crosses to* MAC C) Is he there?

MAC   With his hat off

LEHMAN   What's the low down?

MAC   Built to order. A big butter-and-egg man from the West

LEHMAN   Where'd you get him?

MAC   I'm waiting for this other bird when up blows Sid Bloom with this kid in tow—— He's just a kid   I seen in a minute he was our oyster, and a second later he tells me he's looking to get into show business—— *(Pause   He extends his hands, as though indicating a platter)* With watercress.

LEHMAN. Shoot him in *(Crosses around above desk, sits)* All right, you! *(*JANE *crosses to* R *door, holds it open)* And don't forget that letter stuff *(Sits at desk, feet up)*

MAC Come right in, Mr Jones *(*PETER *enters* R., *hat in hand, rather timidly* PETER *is a boy of twenty-one or so, and it may be said without exaggeration that there are some things he does not know about the world. For the rest, he is simple, likable, and just about average His gaze is on the room at large, and his eyes never go to* JANE WESTON JANE, *however, notices him)* This is Mr. Peter Jones. *(*JANE *exits* R.*)* Mr Lehman, Mr. Jones. *(*R.C*)*

PETER I'm very glad to meet you, Mr. Lehman.

LEHMAN How are you, Sweetheart? *(*PETER *looks behind him)* Sit down *(Takes feet down.* MAC *places chair,* PETER *crosses to desk, sits* R *of desk)* Cigar?

PETER *(Seated* R *of desk,* LEHMAN L. *of desk,* MAC R C.*)* No, thanks

LEHMAN. Where you from?

PETER Chillicothe—— *(Pause)* Ohio.

LEHMAN. Great place. I never played it myself, but they all tell me.

PETER. Mr.—er—this gentleman said you were about to make a theatrical production. *(Looks at* MAC *at* R.C.*)*

LEHMAN I'm doing a wow.

PETER. What?

LEHMAN Listen, Sweetheart—— *(Pulls chair closer)* I got a show that's the greatest dramatic novelty in twenty years There ain't never been nothing like it, see?

MAC *(At* R C*)* I was telling Mr Jones that, providing he acts quick, maybe he could get in on it.

LEHMAN. Ever been in show business, Mr Jones?

PETER Oh, yes We put on two shows last year in Chillicothe—during the hospital drive.

LEHMAN   I see

PETER   During the second one I had charge of everything—told them what to do—the actors   Made over a hundred dollars.

LEHMAN   Well—— *(Leans back and humors him)* Then you know how them things are

PETER   Yes, sir.

LEHMAN   Of course, here in New York, it's just like Mr McClure says—you got to make quick decisions—think on your feet

PETER.   Yes, sir.

MAC   *(Crosses to* PETER*)* There was a friend of ours could have bought in on "Abie's Irish Rose" if he'd snapped it up   He waited 'til the next day and it was too late   *(Crosses away a little)*

LEHMAN   *(Snaps fingers)* That's the show game

PETER   Well, I'm a believer in quick decisions myself, if it's an A-Number-One proposition   Only, of course, I've got to be careful

LEHMAN.   *(Leans back)* Just the kind of man I like, Sweetheart.   What line you been in ?

PETER   I was—in a hotel.

LEHMAN   Working there, you mean—had a job?

PETER   Yes, sir

LEHMAN.   Out in that town?

PETER   Um hm   Chillicothe   (MAC *looks at* PETER *)*

LEHMAN   *(Considers)* This coin—you didn't make it yourself, then?

PETER   No, sir. It was—left me

LEHMAN   How much do you want to put up ?

PETER   *(Pauses)* I'd want to know more about your proposition first. I've got to be careful

LEHMAN   I ain't asking you to go in blindfold *(Puts hat on back of head)* I got a great gag and I ain't afraid to show it   I got a show that's going to catch everybody, see ?   It ain't highbrow and yet it ain't lowbrow

PETER Sort of—medium brow?

LEHMAN. *(Humors him again)* That's it It's the first good medium-brow show they've had, and it's going to be a knockout

PETER How much money do you figure it's going to make?

LEHMAN Say—ask Sam Harris what he's knocking down out of this "Rain" show. Ask that woman what she's making out of "Abie's Irish Rose " Ask Bill Brady what he cleaned up out of "The Man Who Come Back " *(Leans over desk to PETER)*

PETER. You want *me* to ask them?

LEHMAN. I'll tell you, Sweetheart! Millions!

PETER That's what I'd like. Only I'd want it to be safe.

LEHMAN I'll guarantee it personally. So will my friend here. Won't you, Mac?

MAC Sure! *(PETER looks at MAC.)*

LEHMAN Now—what do you say?

PETER Well——

MAC Think on your feet—that's show business.

PETER Oh, I couldn't possibly decide that quickly.

LEHMAN You couldn't?

PETER No, sir I've got to be careful.

LEHMAN Well, when do you think you could decide?

PETER. I'd want to investigate it first. Maybe I could read the play, huh?

LEHMAN. Oh! Well—think we could dig up a script for—— *(PETER looks R. at MAC)* Mr Jones, Mac? *(He shakes his head for MAC to say "no")*

MAC *(Quickly)* No, afraid not. You see, the troupe's in rehearsal, Mr. Jones, and they're using 'em all

LEHMAN I'll show you where it's sure-fire. *(MAC gets chair L Brings it to lower end of desk; sits, back to audience)* Now, look! It's a play about

a dame, see? Only it starts this way. There's a prologue—with a playwright in it, that's in love with
this girl So he asks a bunch of people to come
around and hear him read his new play Now——
(Rises) he starts in to read, and he says, "The first
scene is in an orchard"—and when he says "orchard," instead of his going on reading, we work that
new trick everybody's talking about (PETER *looks
at* MAC)

MAC We call it the "cut-back "

LEHMAN Black out, quick change, lights up, and
it's this orchard Get it?

PETER Um-hm. Just the way he said *(Points to*
MAC)

LEHMAN You got it Then all the rest of it is
his play First, here she is in the orchard——*(Indicates orchard)* only it's the same dame you seen in
the prologue Neat?

PETER You bet

LEHMAN She's younger, see? About seventeen
and playing around the trees. Then along comes
this guy——

PETER. Who?

MAC. The same fellow that was the playwright

LEHMAN He makes love to her, only he's too
nice about it She wants some bozo that'll give her
a lot of hot stuff. You know women. *(Leans over
desk.)*

PETER. Say—— *(Business of hand as if he knew
all about them)*

LEHMAN So this fellow does a getaway and in
blows this other baby. From New York, see, and
dressed sorta loud He gives her an earful about how
beautiful she is, and anyhow, she falls for him

MAC Don't forget the priest.

LEHMAN *(Over desk)* Oh, yeh There's a priest
comes in and there's some gab with him Now ! The

next scene the dame's hitched up to this baby, and having a swell time It's a big cabaret in New York, music and dancing——

MAC. *You* know ! *(Indicates short skirts.)*

LEHMAN. One thing after another happens—anyhow—a guy comes along and insults her. And her husband he says, "What the hell !"—(LEHMAN *backs away)* and back and forth, and out with a gun, and—— *(Snaps fingers, leans over desk)*

PETER. Who does?

MAC. The fellow she's married to croaks the guy that insulted her.

PETER. That's a good thing I'm glad of that

LEHMAN *(Backs away)* Music stops, police,—who done it? *(Bends over desk)* She says she done it.

PETER. But—weren't there a lot of people around at the time?

LEHMAN. Sure they was

PETER Then don't they see the husband shoot him?

LEHMAN No They're all looking the other way *(*PETER *nods.)* And now—comes the trial scene She don't recognize this judge, see?

MAC. He has a beard on.

LEHMAN. Yeh—the judge has got a long beard on—*(Indicates beard)* and she don't—— *(Snaps fingers)* I forgot to tell you this part When she run off with this guy her father kicked her out,— *(*PETER *starts to talk)* see—didn't want no more to do with her, and she ain't seen him since Got it?

PETER Well, I'm not——

LEHMAN *Wait* for the surprise ! A lot of trial stuff, so-and-so and so-and-so and so-and-so—she keeps on saying she done it, and finally this judge he gives her *fifteen years* *(Reads the last part like giving a sentence to some one)*

PETER. Gee ! *(Shakes head)*

LEHMAN   Then—— *(Steps back)* everybody does an exit, she's just there with him, and who does the judge turn out to be but her *own father*. *(Leans over table.)*

PETER   That's a great—coincidence.

MAC.   The father used to be a lawyer.

LEHMAN.   Yeh   Anyhow, it goes back and forth, and she gets crying, and more and more, and goes crazy sorta—and finally they drag her off, cursing like a trooper   That's your first act   *(Starts up* C *)*

PETER.   It's a great start, all right   *(Puts hat on table   LEHMAN takes off coat and throws it up* C *)*

MAC   The name of it is "Her Lesson."

LEHMAN.   *(Crosses down to* C.*)* Yeh—"Her Lesson"   It's a big moral play, see—we get all the women.

PETER   Good

LEHMAN   Second act   Ten years later, and she's just getting out of jail   And she's sore—she's out to get square, and she's doped out a way to skin rich men out of their coin, and still they can't do nothing to her.

MAC   She stays within the law

PETER.   *(Looks at* MAC*)* Say, "Within the Law" would be a good name for a play, wouldn't it?

LEHMAN.   Now!   She's laying plans to fleece a guy that's coming to see her¹   She don't know his name, see?   And *who* does it turn out to be but this other guy that wanted to marry her

PETER   What's he say?

LEHMAN   He gives her a long spiel, and she makes up her mind to go straight   But she can't   She tries it on the next guy and he won't stand for it.   So she says what the hell, and men is all alike, and me for the easiest way.   *(Standing feet slightly apart, palms turned out, hands down)*

PETER.   That was the name of a play.

MAC.   Made half a million.

LEHMAN. Sure fire And now comes the big punch. *(Crosses to* PETER *a little)* Next is the brothel scene. (PETER *pauses, looks at* MAC *)* The dame has been going down hill and there she is, see? Only—before anything terrible can happen, who comes along but this priest. Remember him?

PETER. He used to be in the orchard. *(Points* L *)*

LEHMAN. That's him.

MAC He wants to close this place up.

LEHMAN Of course there's a big scene when he finds the girl in there Everybody's standing around, he opens up on her, then *zowie!*—she comes back at him.

PETER That's fine. I thought she would *(Starts to rise)*

LEHMAN. That's where we bring in the strong talk. She calls him all kinds of names—we go the limit. Then she says, "you priests and missionaries— *(Shakes finger in* PETER's *face)* is all alike. You don't give a girl no chance," and so— *(Backs away to* R *)* and-so and so-and-so and so-and-so—she faints dead away, and somebody says, "Everybody get out of here, she's sick " That's your second act

MAC *(Rises)* Want me to tell the rest?

LEHMAN No!—Act Three is her dream She's delirious, see, and dreams she's dead and gone to Heaven Here's where we got all these angels coming down the aisles——— *(Indicates aisles)*

MAC. With long veils over them

LEHMAN. There was a show done it last year and it was a wow. *(Points up with thumb)* Everything's all mixed up in this act Her father's up there, the Judge, see—only he's supposed to be God.

PETER Is that all right to do?

LEHMAN There was a big *hit* done it. Anyhow, we don't really say it, see?

MAC. Don't forget the priest.

LEHMAN. Oh, yeh This priest comes in and he's

got a rabbi with him, see? And they talk about how everybody's the same underneath, and it doesn't matter none what religion they got Anyhow, just as they're staring to execute her, she wakes up And this fellow, the good one, has got her in his arms, and she says "the bluebird—— *(Hands clasped)* of happiness was at home all the time," kiss, lights out, finishing reading the play, everybody says great, the fellow and the girl gets married, fade out, and curtain. *(Indicates these things* LEHMAN *gets coat and takes it and crosses to* L *of desk)*

MAC. *(Rises, puts chair back* L *and crosses* C *in front of desk)* How do you like it? (LEHMAN *crosses above desk, to* L. *of it Business with coat)*

PETER. My—my—my! I *tell* you Who wrote it?

MAC *(Crosses to* C *)* It used to be a short story.

LEHMAN *(At* L. *of desk)* Yeh, it was a story, see? A story in a highbrow magazine Then some fellow makes a play out of it, a long time ago Only he died, so of course we don't have to pay no royalties. You can't lose with it, Sweetheart. Can you imagine what a picture it'll make for this Swanson baby? *(Leaning over desk to* PETER *)*

PETER Would it take very much money to produce it?

LEHMAN. *(Sits quickly in chair MAC crosses up to end of desk Quickly)* Here's the angle. We're willing to let you half half of it, see—forty-nine per cent

PETER. Of course, I'd be a producer, too?

LEHMAN. Sure. Now—how much was you thinking of putting up?

PETER I'd rather you'd tell me, first.

LEHMAN. I'll let you in on the ground floor. You can have forty-nine percent for—thirty—*(His head comes forward just a little)* thousand dollars

PETER *(Turns in his chair MAC puts his hand*

on his shoulder) Oh, I couldn't think of paying that much.

MAC *(Pleads)* Can't you shave that a little, Joe, for Mr. Jones?

LEHMAN. *(Considers)* I'll tell you what I'll do. Give me a quick Yes and I'll take twenty-five

PETER. I guess we've got to let the whole matter drop. *(He starts to go.)*

LEHMAN. *(Rises and both move as if to stop* PETER*)* Hold on! This coin of yours—you ain't got it some place out West, have you?

PETER. Why?

LEHMAN. Because if it was where you could dig it up in a hurry, maybe we can do business.

PETER. It's right down the street—in a bank *(*LEHMAN *and* MAC *give a sigh of relief.)*

LEHMAN I wasn't going to let it go for this,— *(Sits)* but you give me your check for twenty thousand and forty-nine percent of the show is yours And it's a bargain, ain't it, Mac?

MAC. He couldn't have bought in on "Sally" for that *(Crosses down to* C.)*

LEHMAN And *that* was a big hit, too. Now, what do you say?

PETER. Twenty thousand?

LEHMAN. That's the dope

PETER. Twenty thousand?

LEHMAN. And it's a bargain.

PETER Twenty thousand? *(Faces front, hat in lap.)*

MAC. Think on your feet. (LEHMAN *places hand on pen*)

PETER *(Rises)* Well—I might——

LEHMAN. Set! *(Dips pen in ink,* MAC *crosses above table, takes* PETER'S *hat,* LEHMAN *offers pen quickly,* PETERS *takes pen and sits, starts to write.)*

PETER. It's check number one. (LEHMAN *writes receipt.)*

MAC   *(Looks over* PETER'S *shoulder)* Chatham and Phoenix, eh?

PETER.   Yes, sir.

MAC.   Joe Lehman. L-e-h-m-a-n. *(Crosses* C.*)*

LEHMAN.   *(Making out receipt, tears it out of book and leaves it on blotter)* You're a smart baby, Mr. Jones, and you're going to clean up. (FANNY *starts in* C. *on the last two words.)*

MAC.   Now, just *sign it* *(Crosses down* R *)*

FANNY.   *(Enters angrily up* C *, slams door and crosses down* C. *a little)* Well!

LEHMAN.   Ain't you got no sense at all? Get out of here! Get out of here! *(Up to* C. PETER *partly rises,* MAC *reassures him,* PETER *sits)*

FANNY.   Listen, you four-flushing bum!

LEHMAN.   Now, Fanny—— *(Tries to hush her.)*

MAC   Fanny, for the love of—— *(Indicates to* PETER *to sit down, that it is all right)*

FANNY.   I just come from my bank. And the paying teller says there was a guy around there this morning with black hair and a checked suit and a trick tie trying to find out how big my balance was.

MAC.   Fanny——

LEHMAN.   Now, now, I don't know nothing about it. Come back after a while

FANNY   If you show up around there again they got instructions to shoot on sight. That's all I come to tell you.

MAC.   Don't——

LEHMAN.   Then get out. *(Crosses* L *to upper* L *end of desk and hold)*

FANNY   *(Crosses to* C *door)* I ain't staying! But don't you go snooping around my money, because you ain't going to get a nickel of it! Not for a rotten show like that. *(Exits up* C ; *slams door.)*

(LEHMAN, *cigar in mouth, turns head slowly front.*
PETER *looks after her exit. He looks at* LEH-

MAN *and he gives a sickly smile. Starts to write, then looks around again.* MAC *and* LEHMAN *eye* PETER.*)*

PETER   *(Starts to sign check)* Did she say rotten?

LEHMAN.   She wasn't talking about this show. *(Crosses to* L. *of desk.)*

MAC.   It's another one we got. *(Crosses* L. *to* PETER.*)*

LEHMAN.   She don't even know nothing about this one.

PETER.   Who was it? A friend of yours?

LEHMAN.   My old lady.

PETER.   Oh, your mother, huh?

LEHMAN.   *(Sits* L *of desk)* Now, listen, you got judgment of your own, ain't you? A smart guy like you. I told you about the show. Don't it sound like a wow?

PETER.   But you see—there are reasons why I don't want to lose this money.

LEHMAN.   You ain't going to lose it. Did I tell you about the bookings? *(To* MAC*)* Did I tell him about the bookings?

MAC   Not yet   *(Crosses to back of upper end of desk)*

PETER.   Bookings?

LEHMAN.   The towns we play in—the theatres. *(Takes out route sheet of top drawer in the down end of desk.)*

PETER.   Oh!

LEHMAN   We got the cream. Look! We open in Syracuse. A great show town. And we play there a *full* week.

PETER.   A week, eh?

MAC.   Most shows only get three days

LEHMAN.   Then we go to Providence, Worcester, Albany—all them soft spots.

PETER. I guess they're nice towns, but——
LEHMAN. They're great.
PETER But you see—it's just as I was telling you
—I got a special reason why I wouldn't want to lose
this money—

(JANE *enters* R *, slamming door, with typed paper,*
crosses above desk to LEHMAN, *lays paper on*
desk, smiles at PETER, *exits* R. MAC *takes look*
at paper over LEHMAN'S *shoulder.*)

PETER. *(Eyes* JANE; *hesitates Looks* R. *after her*
exit) Well—would I be working right in this office?
LEHMAN. Sure. Give you a desk right in here
PETER. *(Looks at door* R.) Well—either here or
—out there.
LEHMAN. Whatever you say. (JANE *types out-*
side of door R. PETER *looks at door* R MAC *and*
LEHMAN *exchange looks)*
PETER. *(Signs check As he tears it out of check-*
book LEHMAN *grabs it)* Look out! It's wet!
LEHMAN *(Rises MAC shakes* PETER'S *hand,*
both in hurry to get away) I'll dry it You're a
partner now, Sweetheart *(Hands* PETER *receipt)*
There's your receipt and we'll draw up the papers
later *(Crosses up* C.)
PETER *(Rises)* Wait a minute I guess maybe I
shouldn't have done it.
LEHMAN. *(At* R *of* C *door)* You ain't going to
start worrying?
PETER Shouldn't I?
LEHMAN. I should say not. Now, Mac and me'll
be right back. You wait here, see? Right in this
room *(Crosses up a little)*
PETER. But shouldn't I go with you to the bank?
LEHMAN. You look after things here, see?
PETER. But you see, my check——

MAC. *(Is holding door open, hand on the outside knob They start again)* The bank knows us

PETER But that isn't what I meant. I——

LEHMAN. Now don't worry Just stay right here, because we want to talk to you when we get back, see? I'll tell you what! *(Starts to door R.)*

PETER. What?

LEHMAN *(Calls)* Miss Weston!

PETER. Is that the name of——?

LEHMAN Miss Weston! *(Opens door R)*

MAC. That's her (JANE *enters* R)

LEHMAN. *(At door R.)* Look out for Mr. Jones 'til we come back He's a regular partner *(Starts up* C.) Come on, Mac. *(Exits up* C MAC *looks at* JANE, *exits up* C, *closing door. A pause as* JANE *and* PETER *face each other)*

JANE *(Smiles; is thoroughly at ease)* It wasn't much of an introduction, was it?

PETER I don't mind if you don't.

JANE. *(At* C)* Mr Lehman says you've invested money in the play

PETER. Yes, I—did put some in—a little. *(Picks up checkbook from desk.)*

JANE. I hope it'll be very successful

PETER. *(Rather stiffly)* Thank you *(They come closer together* C)

JANE. I've often wondered how it would feel to be able to do that.

PETER. You mean to be a producer?

JANE Anyhow, to have enough money to be one

PETER. *(Is a bit at a loss as to how to proceed)* It—doesn't feel any way in particular yet. *(Looking at checkbook.)*

JANE. *(At* R.)* Then if I had a *great deal* of money—well, like you—I might go ahead and *be* one

PETER. *(Not quite getting the full implication,*

but coming close enough to be disturbed) How's
that?

JANE   I say, if I could afford to *risk* part of the
money, I'd *be* a producer.

PETER   Risk it? *(Crosses to her a little)* Don't
you think it's a good business, putting plays on?

JANE   Well, of course, it depends. You see——

PETER. *(Grows a little panicky)* But this—this
play of Mr. Lehman's—it's good, isn't it? You
think it'll be a hit? Don't you?

JANE   *(A new doubt has come to her, regards
him)* Tell me something.

PETER   Don't you really?

JANE   *(Now sparring for information)* It—it
will be a hit, of course But—I'm sure you wouldn't
care, would you? A millionaire like you?

PETER. Like me? I'm not anything like that It
was all I could do to—— *(Crosses up around desk
to L of desk)* Well, I hope it turns out all right

JANE   *(Still sizing him up)* You're not a New
Yorker, are you, Mr Jones?

PETER   No, I'm from Chillicothe.

JANE   Oh—you—you haven't been connected
with the theatrical business before, then?

PETER   Oh, yes In a way—we made several productions last year in Chillicothe, sort of.

JANE   *(Sits R. of desk L.C.)* I see.

PETER   It's all right, isn't it? Mr Lehman's play,
I mean? You don't think anything could happen
to it?

JANE   No, it isn't that, but—— *(Leans toward
him)*

PETER   It sounded great, I thought But it'd be
terrible if it wasn't a go

JANE   What I was going to ask you was—of
course it isn't any of my business, but—I was won-
dering how you happened to be here In this office,

I mean. How you ever happened to pick the theatrical business to invest in.

PETER Oh, it's always kind of appealed to me.

JANE *(Pauses)* Did you give Mr Lehman— much money?

PETER Why? There isn't anything the matter, is there? *(Over desk.)*

JANE. No, no. The only reason I asked——

PETER Oh, if there were—— *(Turns head away and back)* Plays do make a lot of money, don't they?

JANE. I'm sure it'll be all right. You mustn't worry.

PETER. All right If you feel that way about it, why—all right

JANE. Well, I—I appreciate your trusting me, of course, but——

PETER Why—you're being here is one of the reasons I went into it Partly.

JANE. How's that?

PETER. I felt pretty sure it was all right or you wouldn't be connected with it at all.

JANE. I'm not sure that I understand

PETER. Well, when you came in—while they were here, you—sort of smiled at me *(She looks away)* Maybe you didn't. I thought you did.

JANE. You did it because I smiled?

PETER I didn't mean——

JANE. Oh, it's all right, only—it just makes me feel a good deal of responsibility, that's all Was it *all* your money that you invested?

PETER Oh, no I've got—some left. A little

JANE Money you'd saved?

PETER. No, we couldn't save much I wasn't earning enough Grandfather had this money he'd saved, and then last June he died. And he left the money to us—mother and me

JANE Was it much?

PETER. Um-huh Twenty-two thousand four hundred dollars.

JANE How much did you invest?

PETER. Well, first I want to tell you You see, if you just take the interest on that, why, it isn't very much to get along on. Because, of course, I wasn't getting very much. Then Mr. Madden—that's the man who owns the hotel—he heard I was getting this money, only he thought it was more,—and he was sort of tired of running the hotel, anyhow—and he said if I could pay him fifty thousand dollars he'd let me have it. It makes a lot of money.

JANE I see

PETE. That's when I thought, if I could take this money we had—and make more out of it, quickly—everything would be fine So, of course, I thought of the theatrical business, because I'd been connected with it, sort of Mother thought too it would be a good thing, and so I left fourteen hundred dollars with her, and I came to New York to look around. That was last week.

JANE. You brought twenty-one thousand with you?

PETER Well, the bank there put it in a bank here for me. So all I had to do was give Mr Lehman a check

JANE. For—all of it?

PETER. Oh, no Only twenty thousand

JANE *(Rises angrily Crosses* C *, looking at door where* LEHMAN *has just left)* Oh!

PETER. What's the matter?

JANE Nothing *(Starts* R *)*

PETER You're not—going, are you?

JANE *(Still half afire with rage at* LEHMAN*)* Yes, I—I think I must

PETER. Thank you very much for coming in and talking to me

JANE *(Turns to him, her mind still half on* LEH-

MAN) I hope again that it's a big success. The play.

PETER. Oh, I feel better about that now, since you talked to me. You see, it's the first time I've talked regularly with anyone since I left home I mean, you're the first person that's—— (MARY MARTIN *enters at* R)

MARTIN. Sorry. Mr Lehman's not here, I see.

JANE. He'll be back soon, Miss Martin

MARTIN. I'm afraid I can't wait. It's important. I told him I was coming back. *(Starts to go; takes hold of doorknob.)*

PETER. Is it—*(Crosses to* R *of desk)*—something to do with the firm?

MARTIN. How's that? *(Stops at door.)*

PETER. I say, if it's something to do with the firm, maybe I can do it for you.

MARTIN. Oh! *(Crosses to* PETER C *)* I wonder if this is the young man Mr Lehman spoke about? That was—coming into the company?

PETER Yes, ma'am

MARTIN Oh—then of course you can do it *(Dismisses* JANE *with a look.* JANE *starts to go)*

PETER. You needn't go, Miss Weston

JANE. *(Opens door)* I will, if you don't mind. *(Exits* R *)*

MARTIN. *(Crossing to* PETER*)* I don't believe Mr. Lehman mentioned your name.

PETER Jones, Peter Jones.

MARTIN. I'm Mary Martin, Mr Jones *(She puts her hand out and he takes it)* I'm with the show.

PETER Really? Our show?

MARTIN. Yes So you and I will probably see a good deal of each other

PETER We will, huh?

MARTIN Oh, indeed, yes

PETER *(Pauses, embarrassed)* Which one are you? In the show—— *(Let go of hands)* I mean?

MARTIN   Oh, the lead.

PETER   The what?

MARTIN   The leading part

PETER. Oh, yes, that's a great role   I mean, she gets in a lot of trouble.

MARTIN. I hope you're coming to rehearsals soon, Mr. Jones   I'm sure we will want to get your ideas.

PETER   My ideas?

MARTIN. Of course   I do particularly.

PETER. Oh, I don't know that I'd be much good at——

MARTIN   You'd be wonderful   *(Looks at him)* And I can tell

PETER   Oh, I did make a few productions out in Chillicothe.

MARTIN. *(Flatters him)* There, you see! I knew the minute I saw you   Now I want you to promise you'll come to rehearsals and that whenever you have any suggestions for me you'll tell me

PETER   All right.

MARTIN. *(Crosses to C)* I can't tell you how relieved I am that you've come in to take charge of things

PETER   Oh, I'm not going to take charge

MARTIN   Oh, yes, you will   *(Snaps fingers as if remembering something)* I knew there was something, Mr Jones   *(Crosses to PETER)* I wonder if you'd do me a very great favor?

PETER. Yes, ma'am

MARTIN. I don't like to trouble you, but I left my checkbook at home this morning   And just now I saw the darlingest frock and they won't *hold* it *(Puts on air)*

PETER. Why—that's all right   *(Sits R of desk, starts to write check.)*

MARTIN   That's lovely of you   I hate to *bother* you   It will be taken out of my salary   Just a hundred. *(Looking over his shoulder)*

PETER Just a hundred. *(Starts to write a check.)*

MARTIN Just make it to cash. I think it's wonderful, your coming in with us, Mr. Jones. It makes everything seem so different. *(After he finishes and tears check out)* Oh, that's just fine. *(He rises and blots check on desk pad)* I'm ever so much obliged. *(Takes check)* Thank you.

PETER. You're welcome.

MARTIN. Now, don't forget You're coming to rehearsals And you're going to tell me just what you think.

PETER. There was something—when they were— Oh—I was thinking, a little while ago—that is, if you're sure you don't mind?

MARTIN. Mind? I'm crazy for suggestions. *(Backing away from him to R C)*

(WARN Curtain)

PETER You know that part where you're in— that place?

MARTIN. Place? I'm not sure just which scene—

PETER You know. The place—that you go to—?

MARTIN. You don't mean the Heaven scene?

PETER. No, ma'am Just before the Heaven scene.

MARTIN Oh, the brothel.

PETER Yeh *(Coming C)* That's the place. That's where, if I were you, I'd really do some of my best acting—where you bring in the strong talk— "You priests and missionaries are no better than a lot of rabbis——"

MARTIN Oh, yes—indeed I will, Mr. Jones. *(Puts check in purse)* And thank you.

PETER You're welcome. I'll come to rehearsals myself tomorrow.

MARTIN I can go out this way, can't I? *(Starts up C.)*

PETER. Yes, ma'am. *(Opens door C.)*

MARTIN It's been a great pleasure, Mr. Jones.

PETER. It has been for me, too.

MARTIN   *(They shake hands)* Something tells me we're going to be very good friends   Because I know you'll produce other plays, too, won't you ?

PETER.   I don't know

MARTIN   Of course you will—a man like you.

PETER   Well, maybe a couple

MARTIN.   And now, good-bye until tomorrow And I want to tell you what a pleasure it is to be under your management   Good-bye   *(Exits to R)*

PETER.   Good-bye   *(As he stands in door looking after her he puts left hand to head in a nervous manner, as if he had just passed through a great strain He looks at name on the outside of the door, closes door, looks at name on door inside, satisfied, looks about room, feels desk, crosses down, looks at route sheet, sits in chair, tries it, then forgets and leans back and chair goes back with him, giving him a start; pulls chair closer, puts on hat, puts feet on desk, then tips hat forward over eyes)*

CURTAIN

ACT II

SCENE I: *A hotel room in Syracuse, shortly before the curtain rings up on "Her Lesson" It is in all respects a typical hotel room, from the heavy maroon hangings on the windows to the picture of the signing of the Declaration of Independence on the wall There is but a single door, set in an alcove up left, and when it swings wide enough you can read the room number, 726 Across the outside hall the edge of another door is barely visible*

The room is our hero's, of course. Being the gentleman who made the production possible, he has been favored with ample quarters At the right are two windows, and between them a dresser. Set in the rear wall, toward the right, is a clothes closet, adjoining it on the left is a chiffonier, and then comes the inevitable bed, set at right angles to the footlights. There is a writing-table against the wall at left, there are two or three small chairs and one more comfortable.

It is evening—eight o'clock or thereabouts

PETER *discovered in evening dress, tie around collar but not tied. Dress coat hanging on hall tree up* R C. *He has dress vest on. He is standing down* R C., *and as the curtain rises crosses hurriedly up stage to closet up* R.C. *and hangs up top coat which he has already on a hanger to save time. Comes out of closet and shuts door; starts for dresser* R.

LEHMAN *knocks off up* L.

40

PETER. Come in! (PETER *starts to tie tie at dresser.*)

LEHMAN. *(Enters up L. Same clothes as Act I)* How are you, Sweetheart? *(Crosses down L C.)*

PETER. Oh, hello. *(Turns, then crosses to LEHMAN)* I was looking for you.

LEHMAN *(Noticing dress clothes)* Say!

PETER Aren't the—rest of them doing it? *(Crosses R C)*

LEHMAN *(Crosses to foot of bed)* That don't make no difference How's the kid? *(Sits at foot of bed)*

PETER I thought—being an opening——

LEHMAN Sure! And it's going to be some opening. The biggest Syracuse has ever seen.

PETER *(Crosses to LEHMAN at foot of bed)* Well, then look What I wanted to say was—if a lot of people come to see it this week—and they will, won't they?

LEHMAN We'll be turning 'em away.

PETER. Then would it be possible for you, before we leave here, to let me have a little money back? Just some of the profits?

LEHMAN. *(Rises from bed)* I'll tell you, Sweetheart, this is sort of an expensive show, see? We might be out on the road a couple of weeks before we really start cleaning up Big, I mean

PETER You won't—have any money here?

LEHMAN. Not to split up But don't you worry none about your coin If this show ain't a hit, I'll eat it.

PETER Well, as long as I get some pretty soon— *(Starts R. for dresser and has hold of tie as if to tie it.)*

LEHMAN Sure you will *(Looks at watch)* Ready? Pretty near curtain—*(Crosses L.)* time.

PETER. Why—just about *(Crosses back to LEH-*

MAN*)* I don't suppose you could tie a bow tie, could you, Mr. Lehman?

LEHMAN. *(Comes back to* c.*)* Afraid not.

PETER. Well, I'll try it again. *(Crosses to dresser* R *and starts to tie the tie again.)*

MAC. *(Enters up* L *)* Are you coming? How are you, Mr. Jones? *(Crosses to* LEHMAN *down* C *)*

PETER. Oh, hello *(Looks around to* MAC *)*

LEHMAN. What room's Weston in?

MAC. Down the way. You want her?

LEHMAN Yeh. And tell Fanny I'm here in twenty-six.

MAC. O K. *(Exits up* L. *to* L. *hurriedly)*

LEHMAN. *(Looks around room)* Oh—er—the reason I come in, Sweetheart—you got such a nice big room, I thought maybe you wouldn't mind if we was to get together up here after the show

PETER *(Faces* LEHMAN *but stands at dresser, still holding ends of tie)* Tonight?

LEHMAN. Sure.

PETER. You mean—to celebrate? *(Lets go of tie)*

LEHMAN. Well—sort of talk things over There might be some changes or something.

PETER. Changes—— *(Crosses* R C *toward* LEHMAN) in the play?

LEHMAN In case there is any

PETER Isn't it all right?

LEHMAN Great But there might be something, see? Just a line.

PETER Oh!

LEHMAN I and the wife is cooped up in twenty-eight, next door—but this is good and big so we can all get in.

PETER All who?

LEHMAN Well—whoever comes You see, after a show's opened you always have a sort of conference—talk it over.

PETER   You mean for me to be here too, don't you?

LEHMAN.   Sure   We'll want to know what everybody *thinks,* see?   *(A couple of steps to* PETER*)*   I'll tell you—you take a wad of paper at the show tonight and put down anything you see that's wrong

PETER   Anything about the play?

LEHMAN   Play, acting, scenery, anything.   Make a note of it—then we'll talk it over

PETER   What I thought you did after a play has opened is—sort of have a supper, and celebrate.

LEHMAN   We can do that, too   Great.

PETER   I'd like that   Miss Weston could come, couldn't she?

LEHMAN   Sure.   You invite her   *(Crosses to* L C *)*

PETER   *(Crosses to* LEHMAN *)*   And don't they usually——   Do you think they'd let us have some champagne?   If I asked them

LEHMAN   I'll introduce you to the manager   Only look out for him—he's show-crazy.

PETER.   He's what?

LEHMAN   Show-crazy   Off his nut about show business.

PETER.   Why?

LEHMAN   *(Starts for door* U L *)*   Are you coming?

JANE   *(Enters up* L. PETER *sees* JANE, *crosses up to hat tree quickly and puts on dress coat)*   Yes, Mr. Lehman?   *(Down to* LEHMAN L.C *)*

LEHMAN   Oh!   I want you right beside me during the play, see?   Take notes as I dictate 'em   We're going right over   (MAC *crosses past door, going from* R *to* L *in hall)*   Mac——   *(Exits up* L *)*

JANE   *(At* U L *)*   Very well   *(Turns to go)*

PETER   Oh, Miss Weston!   *(At hat tree up* R.C *)*   Miss Weston.

JANE   Hello.

PETER. *(Crosses to* R C *)* Would you come to a sort of party tonight, here in this room, to celebrate the success of the show? There'll be other people here.

JANE. Why—of course. I'd be delighted. *(Starts out.)*

PETER. Please don't go yet. I haven't seen you for a long time, to talk to at all. I almost thought you—didn't want to talk to me.

JANE. Why shouldn't I want to talk to you? *(Hold up by door)*

PETER. Won't you, for a minute now, then? The —door's open—that makes it all right.

· JANE *(Looks toward door)* I think Mr Lehman wants me soon.

PETER. He'll call for you again—— *(*JANE *comes down to foot of bed)* You haven't said anything to me about the play, and it's the opening night. I'm a producer. *(Crosses to foot of bed* R.*)*

JANE I wish you the best of luck

PETER Thanks

JANE I can't bear to think of its being anything but a—great success.

PETER. Neither can I It's bound to be, don't you think?

JANE. Well—remember, if it isn't just perfect to-night, it can probably be fixed

PETER. I'm going to take notes of whatever's wrong.

JANE That's right.

PETER *(Crosses up to her)* Look—I didn't want to ask Mr. Lehman about this, but you don't think there's any chance of—my having to make a speech, do you—tonight?

JANE. I—don't—think so.

PETER I didn't really think there was, but—just in case it should happen—that was the reason I wore this. One of the reasons *(Indicates dress suit.)*

JANE. I see.

PETER. Oh, look! *(Notices tie still undone)* Can you tie a bow tie?

JANE. *(Crosses to him at foot of bed)* Why, yes— *(Does so)*

PETER You see, at home my mother always did it for me when I wore it. I only wore it once. They gave a big dance at the hotel We had it all fixed up—— Oh, it was beautiful——

JANE. There! *(Finishes tie.)*

PETER. Is it finished? Thanks. *(Looks at her)* Oh—wait a minute. *(Gets roses in box from closet U R)* I got these for you for tonight on account of the opening

JANE Oh! Why—that was lovely of you *(She takes box)*

PETER *(Points to box as he steps back a few steps)* They're flowers.

JANE *(Puts box on bed, takes off cover)* They're beautiful. *(She takes them in her arms and faces PETER)* You shouldn't have done that.

PETER Well, on account of the opening, and besides—I wanted to. You know, you look awfully lovely with them—I mean—the way you're standing there—and the way—— Gosh! *(JANE puts flowers in box on bed with a sudden gesture)* What's the matter?

JANE. I'm the last person—that you should give flowers to.

PETER Last—why, you're the first. You're the only one I want to give any to—the only one I ever wanted to give any to That's—the truth

JANE I can't let you say those things.

PETER *(A few steps to her)* But I can't help it And I've got to say something more I—I've just got to I want to know whether—some day—you think you could ever—marry a theatrical producer?

JANE Please——

PETER   I don't mean just a producer with forty-nine percent of one show—but there'll come a time when I'll have my own theatre—and——

JANE.   Peter, don't! You're going to hate me! Just—hate me!

(WARN Curtain)

PETER   Not much. I'm going—to love you I do now, Jane That's what I've been trying to get at—

JANE   Please——

PETER   Only I guess—I know it's kind of nervy of me, but——

LEHMAN.   *(Enter up L from L)* How about you in there? Ready? (MAC *enters up L. after LEH-MAN from L)*

PETER.   I'll get my things. *(Starts for closet up R)*

JANE   I'll be at the theatre *(Starts for door up L)*

PETER.   *(Stops)* Aren't you going with us?

JANE.   I've some things—to attend to—if you don't mind. *(Exits up L)*

PETER.   Well, I'll see you over there *(Enters closet for cane, silk hat and top coat.)*

LEHMAN.   Ready?

PETER   Yes, sir *(Comes out of closet with top coat over left arm, cane in left hand, silk hat in right hand)* Well, here we go

LEHMAN   Right! And it's going to be a big night! Come along! *(Starts L.)*

PETER.   Shouldn't we wish each other—good luck, or something?

LEHMAN   *(Stops)* Why, of course *(Crosses to PETER, and shakes hands)* Good luck, Mr. Jones!

PETER.   Good luck to you! (LEHMAN *crosses L)*

MAC   *(At R C   Crosses to PETER)* Good luck! *(Shakes hands with PETER)*

PETER   Good luck to you, Mr McClure!

LEHMAN.   *(At L)* A whale of a hit, Sweetheart!

That's what we're going to have—a whale of a hit!
    MAC   You bet we are! *(Slaps* PETER *on back)*
Aren't we?
    PETER   Yes, sir! A whale of a hit! *(Puts on silk
hat)* Sweetheart. *(Swings cane and starts out   As
he takes about two steps, ring Curtain   LEHMAN
starts out first, followed by* MAC, *then* PETER *)*

CURTAIN

ACT II

SCENE II: *Curtain down only a few seconds, providing for the lapse of several hours When it rises the room is in near darkness—only a small lamp on the bed table is lighted Immediately the sound of a key is heard in the door. The door opens, and for a second the figure of* PETER, *stick, high hat and all, is silhouetted against the brightly lighted hallway He presses the lights on, leaves the door open behind him and comes into the room, whistling gaily Still whistling, he hangs up his coat* LEHMAN, *a disconsolate figure with hands in pockets and eyes on the floor, comes slowly into the room He is followed, at a respectful distance, by* MAC—*a much repressed* MAC LEHMAN *drops onto the bed, with a sigh, and* MAC *slumps into the chair at the writing table* PETER *is vastly puzzled He regards them for a second, then finally gets up courage to ask* LEHMAN *a question.*

PETER. Is something the matter? I thought it was all right Except—here and there, maybe

LEHMAN. *(Rises, crosses to chair* R *)* Oh—— *(Sits.)*

PETER Isn't it any good at all?

FANNY *(Enters up* L *, clears throat, crosses to* C *and plants herself)* First——

LEHMAN. *(Rises)* Now, one thing we ain't going to have none of is wisecracks They can't nobody tell me we ain't got a great show—when it's fixed *(WAITER starts to enter off* L *in hall)* Just because

48

this bunch tonight give us the raspberry don't prove nothing. Syracuse is the bummest show town in the world.

WAITER   *(Arrives down* L C *with tray on left shoulder, six wine glasses, three knives, three forks, three plates, service table in right hand)* Is this where the party's going to be? *(Looking at* FANNY *)*

FANNY. *(Crosses to foot of bed)* Party is right.

PETER. *(Turns to* WAITER*)* If you'll just bring the things——

WAITER   Yes, sir. *(Crosses up* R.C. *and puts tray on serving table)*

PETER   *(Turns back to* LEHMAN*)* It's just a little thing, isn't it—the matter? I mean, the play's a success?

WAITER. *(Crosses down to* PETER *at his* L *)* Mr. Fritchie says he'll be up later to see if everything is all right

PETER   What?

WAITER. Mr Fritchie, the assistant manager. He says——

LEHMAN. Never mind

WAITER   *(Looks at* LEHMAN*)* Yes, sir. *(Exits up* L. *to* L *)*

LEHMAN. All I need is that nut.

FANNY   *(Sarcastic apology)* May I ask a question? *(At* C *)*

LEHMAN   Go easy with me

FANNY   Are you going to put anything in that five-minute spot where Martin couldn't think of the next line?

PETER   *(At* R *)* Oh, yes I noticed that.

FANNY. Because if she's going to wait like that every night I figure it'd be a great place for a specialty   I could come on with the clubs—— *(Crosses up* C *to chiffonier.)*

LEHMAN. I know you don't like her. Now lay

off! Did you tell that ham Director we was meeting here?

MAC. Be here any minute.

LEHMAN. How about Bernie—is he ever coming?

MAC. I give him the room

LEHMAN. And where's Weston with them notes? I don't get no co-operation.

MAC. I'll get her *(Crosses up L.)*

PETER Here are my notes, Mr. Lehman, if—— *(At R.)*

LEHMAN Better give Bernie a ring—get him up here.

MAC. Right *(Exits up L. off to R)*

LEHMAN Was he at the show? I didn't see him.

FANNY I saw him *(Up C)*

LEHMAN. What did he say? *(She starts to speak)* Don't tell me

PETER Mr Lehman,— *(Crosses down to him at LEHMAN'S L.)* here are the notes that I put down, if——

LEHMAN What?—Oh——

JANE *(Enters up L from R with notes and Mss. and notebook, pencil)* Did you want me, Mr. Lehman? *(MAC re-enters up L. from R to 'phone)*

LEHMAN *(Takes off coat and throws it on foot of bed)* Give me them notes. And bring that table over here to the light *(Indicates writing-table against wall L.)*

PETER Wait a minute I'll get it. *(Does so.)*

MAC. Kitty, give me four thirteen. *(Short pause)* How'd you like the show? *(This to the 'phone operator.)*

PETER *(To JANE)* How'd you like it? *(As he carries table.)*

(WAITER *enters up L. with two bottles of wine in two coolers, places one on each side of serving-table.)*

LEHMAN   Hey—hey—— *(Sets table* R *with enough room for a chair between the* R *of table and* FANNY'S *chair, which is also* R. *As* PETER *gets table placed at* R, LEHMAN *puts chair he has just taken from* R *corner and puts it above table* PETER *sees this chair and takes it and puts it* R *of table for* JANE *and she sits.* LEHMAN *gives* PETER *a look* PETER *crosses to* L *again and gets the other chair for* LEHMAN; *he sits.)*

MAC   *(On the 'phone)* Well, I wouldn't go as far as that   *(This speech is read through the above business)* Of course we've got a little work ahead   You got to make allowances for it being an opening   By the time it reaches the big burg we'll have it clicking all along the line

LEHMAN.   *(To* JANE*)* Now—you take down anything that—(PETER *comes down to* JANE*)* comes up, see?   *(To* PETER*)* Let her alone   (WAITER *has arranged glasses on tray*)

FANNY   *(Picks up wine bottle at* L. *of serving-table)* Well, now, who did all this?

PETER   Huh?   *(Crosses up* R C *)* Oh, it's to celebrate the success of the show   It's champagne.

FANNY   *(To* PETER*)* Do they open?

PETER   Yes, ma'm

FANNY.   Soon?

PETER   Oh, excuse me.   Ah—waiter—open some champagne

WAITER   (FANNY *hands* WAITER *bottle)* Yes, sir   *(Opens bottle   Fills glass nearest* FANNY *first*)

MAC   *(In 'phone)* Bernie?—Mac——

LEHMAN   Tell him to hurry up

MAC   We're getting together up here in seven twenty-six, whenever you're ready—O K   *(Hangs up   Crosses down* L   WAITER *fills two other glasses with wine*)

FANNY   I don't like to seem in a hurry, but you

see, I saw all three acts. *(Picks up glass of wine*
WAITER *gives her a look as he finishes pouring third
glass.)*

LEHMAN. *(To* JANE*)* Where's all them second-
act notes? Lose 'em? (WAITER *puts bottle under
serving-table in cooler* L*, cork out)*

JANE   No, sir   They're right here.

LEHMAN.   Oh!

PETER. *(Crosses down* R. *to* JANE*)* Will anyone
else—have some champagne? Miss Weston? (WAIT-
ER *takes cork out of second bottle,* R. *of serving-
table, but leaves it in cooler.)*

JANE   No, thank you.

LEHMAN. *(To* FANNY*)* You're beginning that,
huh? Is that—(WAITER *starts* L *)*—Director coming or ain't he? And where's Bernie?

MAC   They'll be along.

WAITER   *(Stops* L C. *To* PETER*)* Mr. Fritchie
says—how soon do you want the food served?

PETER   *(Crosses to* WAITER, L C *)* Oh, yes   Do
you want the food served right away? Chicken a la
King

LEHMAN   I don't care   Only keep that nut Fritchie away from here

WAITER   (PETER *starts to speak)* Yes, sir   *(Exits
up* L *off to* L *)*

FANNY   *(Toast)*   To Mary, Queen of Stage
Waits. *(Takes wine bottle in* L. *hand and glass of
wine in right, crosses to big chair at* R *; chair has
arms wide enough to put glasses of wine on)*

LEHMAN. *(At* C *)* Will you shut that door——?
Now where is everybody? I don't get no co-operation, that's the trouble   I pay a director three hundred a week—where is he? I bring Bernie Sampson
up from New York—where is he?

PETER. *(Down to* LEHMAN*)* Three hundred dollars, did you give him? (BENHAM *knocks door up
L.)*

LEHMAN. (FANNY *pours drink, standing in front of chair*) Answer that, will you?

PETER. Who—me? *(Starts up FANNY sits down R in chair.)*

LEHMAN *(At R C., crosses to table, bends over papers)* If you don't mind (PETER *opens the door CECIL BENHAM enters.)* Thank God! What the hell happened to that scenery?

BENHAM *(A calm, reserved and dignified Englishman, who is even able to wear a monocle without suggesting musical comedy Coming down L C, hat in hand)* I beg your pardon?

LEHMAN. I said, what happened to the scenery? It was crooked—all through the show.

PETER *(At L C)* I got a note of that

BENHAM. My dear Mr Lehman, I was hardly in position to prevent that.

LEHMAN You're the director, ain't you?

BENHAM Permit me to point out that not even a director can be everywhere You may not realize it, but I was holding book all evening

PETER. *(To MAC at L)* What was he holding? (MAC *explains by pantomime*)

LEHMAN. Oh! Well, if you were holding book, where were you during that stage wait of Martin's in the second act? Couldn't you throw her the line?

BENHAM I gave Miss Martin the line four times. She seemed to be nervous.

PETER. *(Crosses to C, between BENHAM and LEHMAN)* She wasn't feeling well.

LEHMAN What?

PETER I say, she told me she wasn't feeling well

LEHMAN When did you see her?

PETER In her dressing room between the acts. I was giving her some notes

LEHMAN *You* were?

PETER Yes, sir.

LEHMAN Well, for the—— *(A knock on the*

door U L. LEHMAN *controls himself)* Answer that, will you? (PETER *goes up* BENHAM *crosses up and sits on* L *of bed.)* If that's Bernie, we can get at this. (PETER *opens door.* BERNIE *enters up* L, *straw hat on, street suit)*

MAC It's Bernie. (PEGGY *enters up* L *after* BERNIE *and at his* L, *cigarette in holder)*

BERNIE (BERNIE SAMPSON *is a slightly Semitic young man with that air of sophistication about him that can be acquired only through long service on Broadway* PEGGY MARLOWE *is a smartly dressed and ever so good-looking chorus girl)* Hello, people. Hello, Joe.

LEHMAN Hello!

BERNIE How are you, Mackie?

MAC Hello!

BERNIE Come on, baby. I just happened to have a young lady with me (BENHAM *rises, leaves hat on bed, stands by bed)*

MAC That's all right. (LEHMAN *sits at table* R C)

BERNIE. *(At foot of bed)* This is Miss Marlowe, folks.

PEGGY *(*R *of* MAC, *down* L) How are you? *(Nods, blowing out cloud of smoke)*

MAC (PETER *comes down* L) Let's see. This is Mrs Lehman—Mr Lehman—Mr Benham— (BENHAM *up* L C) and Mr. Jones. (PETER *at* L)

FANNY *(On "Mrs Lehman")* Hi——

PEGGY *(Looks coldly about room)* Aren't there any chairs in this dump? *(Starts to walk slowly to* R *of bed)*

BERNIE (BENHAM *crosses up by suitcase* L) Sit on the bed *(He tosses hat on bed)*

PEGGY Sit on it yourself. *(Crosses to* R *of bed, takes off coat and tosses it on* C *of bed)*

PETER I'm sorry—there don't seem to be any more chairs. Maybe——

MAC. Mr. Jones, will you run into my room and get some—twenty-two—the door's open. (PEGGY *walks slowly to serving-table up* R C *)*

PETER Well—don't decide anything 'til I come back. *(Exits up* L *off* L *)*

PEGGY Well, if it isn't my old friend, liquor. *(Picks up glass of wine and drinks, and holds position)*

LEHMAN (BENHAM *crosses to* L *corner of bed)* Now, Bernie, I want you to tell us just what you think of it. (PEGGY *takes off hat, looks in mirror* R , *but holds her position by tray* LEHMAN *to* BEN-HAM, *who is at foot of bed)* Mr Sampson here came up from New York to see the show, and maybe do some work if it needs it

BENHAM Is that so? (PEGGY *picks up knife and fork from serving-table up* R C *)*

LEHMAN Now, we're all going to give our frank opinions, see?

FANNY *(Starts to rise)* Well—

LEHMAN That's enough! *(Puts hand up to* FANNY*)* Bernie, you're first. (BENHAM *crosses over* L *To* JANE*)* Take this down. (PEGGY *starts down to* R *of* BERNIE *)*

PEGGY *(Holds up knife and fork)* Does anything go with these? *(To* BERNIE *)*

LEHMAN Shut up! Oh—I thought it was Fanny. (PEGGY *turns quickly to* LEHMAN, *then away to the tray, and then sits on bed)* All right, Bernie.

BERNIE *(At* C *foot of bed)* Well, I'll tell you—

PETER *(Enters up* L *with two chairs from* L *)* Was anything decided?

LEHMAN. Will you shut that door, please? (PETER *puts chairs down* L C, *crosses up, shuts door up* L. MAC *takes chair, sits astride it at* L BENHAM *takes the other, sits and smokes cigarette on* MAC'S R. *Chairs close together.)* Bernie! Go ahead!

BERNIE *(At* C *)* Well, of course there ain't no

doubt but what it needs some work. Now, when I catch a show I don't look at the show so much. I look at the audience. They'll tell you every time. Now, your prologue is great. (MAC *and* PETER *pleased*) It's a great idea—him reading the play. And it held 'em. It's a novelty. But after that they begun to slip away from you.

PETER *(To* BERNIE*)* I'd like to talk to you about that. *(Crosses to* BERNIE *at* C *)*

BERNIE Who's the kid? *(Turns to* PETER.*)*

LEHMAN If you don't mind, Mr. Jones.

PETER Well, I just wanted to talk to him——

LEHMAN. All right! Go on, Bernie! (PETER *crosses back of* BERNIE *to* R. *of* BERNIE, *up* R C *)*

BERNIE Well, I'll tell you. Some of them scenes —they don't click *(He snaps his fingers)* Now I got a scene,—— (PEGGY *crosses to* L *of* PETER*)* that I done in a show called—ah——

PEGGY Hello, Cutie—— *(At* PETER'S L *)*

PETER. Hello.

BERNIE *(To* PEGGY *and* PETER*)* Say, what's going on here?

PEGGY Mind your business

LEHMAN Bernie, can't you get rid of her somehow?

PEGGY. Let him try! What I got on him! (BERNIE *nervous business.* PEGGY *turns and looks at* PETER *)*

LEHMAN Are we going to get anything done here, or ain't we?

FANNY I vote "no." *(Pours wine)*

LEHMAN Go ahead, Bernie—you was saying?

BERNIE Well—if this kid's going to butt in. *(Eyes* PETER.*)*

PETER I was just listening. (FANNY *drinks)*

LEHMAN. Oh—go on, Bernie. (PEGGY *sits on* R. *of bed)*

BERNIE Where was I?

LEHMAN. You was saying you got a scene

BERNIE. Oh, yah You got to put something in the place of that cabaret scene Of course, it may be the way it was put on. I don't know who done it for you, but of all the lousy directing—

BENHAM *(Rises, crosses to* BERNIE*)* I beg your pardon, Mr. Jackson.

MAC *(To* BENHAM*)* Now, that's all right.

BERNIE (MAC *stands between the two* C *)* Bernie Sampson is my name.

BENHAM It's quite possible that you don't know who I *am.*

BERNIE. That's only part of it.

BENHAM I was associated for ten years with Sir John Hare, and I've been with Sir Charles Wyndham and Sir Beerbohm Tree.

FANNY *(Looks at* BENHAM*)* And where are they now ?

BENHAM I am not accustomed to having my direction described by that adjective. (FANNY *drinks)*

BERNIE. Listen, I come up from New York as a favor to Joe here——

BENHAM. Nevertheless, I must insist——

LEHMAN Now don't let's get scrapping.

BENHAM But if he's to be permitted——

MAC. *(Between* BERNIE *and* BENHAM*)* Now, there's no use flying off the handle—— *(Holds* BENHAM *back)*

BENHAM Yes, but—but——

MAC He didn't mean anything *(Pushing* BENHAM *in chair* L *)*

BENHAM. Well—I—— *(Sits)*

MAC That's the stuff

PEGGY Is that going to be all?

BERNIE Now, baby——

PEGGY. Well—call me if it gets good. *(Lies on bed)*

LEHMAN Go on, Bernie.

BERNIE. *(A nod of head toward* BENHAM*)* What's this guy so touchy about?

BENHAM *(Starts to rise.* MAC *lays a restraining hand on his shoulder)* Well——

LEHMAN *(To* BERNIE*)* Never mind, Bernie! What's this scene you got?

BERNIE Well, I'll tell you. It'll drop right in where your cabaret is, see? It was a wow scene, but the show never come to New York, so it'll be new. There's never been anything like it. It was a hop joint in Hongkong.

BENHAM *(With great dignity)* It would not possibly do.

LEHMAN We got to stick to the story, Bernie. We can't throw away the whole play.

FANNY Why not? *(Drinks at end of laugh* BERNIE *crosses up* R.C. *between bed and serving-table)*

LEHMAN. Now, I'll tell you. Suppose we start at the beginning—— *(*FANNY *puts glass on arm of chair.* MARTIN *knocks at door up* L. PETER *crosses* L *to door)*

LEHMAN Who's this?

FANNY. Oh—you can't tell. *(*PETER *opens door.* MARTIN *enters up* L., *walks down* L C *as* FANNY *applauds Stops and gives* FANNY *a dirty look.* FANNY *applauds and rests head on hand)*

MARTIN *(At* C.*)* Now, before anything is said—that stage wait was not my fault.

LEHMAN. All right, all right. *(*PETER *crosses to* R *of bed again)*

MARTIN Maxwell gave me the wrong cue—a cue out of the third act So, of course, I had to stop and think.

FANNY. *(Rises a little and leans on arm of chair)* Well, you certainly had a lovely evening for it.

MARTIN. *(Turns to* BENHAM *at* L *)* And then——

you'd think there'd be someone in the wings to throw
me a line. But no.

BENHAM   That's not true, *(Rises)* Miss Martin. I gave you the line distinctly.

MARTIN   *(Angry)* Well, I certainly didn't hear
it. *(Crosses to* BENHAM *)*

PEGGY   *(Sitting up)* Oh, goody, a scrap——
(Then sits up on bed)

LEHMAN. Now, stop——

MARTIN   (PETER *gets up* R C *, above* LEHMAN,
R *of* MARTIN*)* Besides—I've had a raging head-
ache all day. And if you think it's easy to give a
performance of a *star* part, with people coming back
into your dressing-room all the time—*(She eyes*
PETER*)* trying to tell you what to do—— (ALL *eye*
PETER *and he backs away a couple of steps)*

PETER   You said if I had any suggestions——
*(*FANNY *nearly finishes glass of wine)*

MARTIN.   Well, really, Mr Jones—I've been in
the profession longer than you have

FANNY.   *(Drops arm and glass over* R *arm of
chair, holds glass)* And that's no fairy tale

MARTIN.   (BERNIE *takes* PEGGY'S *cigarette and
puts ashtray on chiffonier* BENHAM *sits in same
chair again.* MARTIN *is angry)* I beg your pardon!
*(*MAC *crosses up and puts cigarette on 'phone table)*

LEHMAN   *(Rises)* Oh, stop it—you two! Sit
down, Mary. (MARTIN *takes chair* L *and turns back
on* BENHAM *and* BENHAM *does the same)* Now—
(Looks at papers) We're going to begin at the beginning and go right through the show.

MAC   *(Crosses down* L C*)* Joe—do you want
some good, straight dope? A fresh viewpoint?

LEHMAN   Who?

MAC   There's a little girl down on the switchboard, smart as a steel trap   She sees everything
that comes here, and I slipped her a couple tonight.
Now——

LEHMAN. Good idea. Get her up. Anybody but that nut Fritchie. *(Sits at table R C.)*

MAC. Right!

PEGGY. Did he say on the switchboard? *(Crosses down R.C. to L. of LEHMAN. MAC talks pantomime at 'phone)*

BERNIE. Now, baby——

PEGGY. Is there more than one operator in this hotel?

BERNIE Never mind.

PEGGY. Because I just had a run-in with one of them and I'd like to know.

LEHMAN. Bernie—can't you get this dame to sit down or something?

BERNIE Some other time, baby——

PEGGY Well—just in case she *is* the one, I'll take another drink. *(PETER hands her glass; she takes drink)*

MAC *(During last seven lines, above, but sotto voce)* Kitty? This is Mr. McClure—Jack. Can you leave there for a minute and come to seven twenty-six? I'll tell you when you get here—— That's right. Thanks. *(Hangs up on PEGGY's word "drink" BERNIE gets PEGGY to sit on bed)*

LEHMAN Now—pleasee. We ain't going to have no more interruptions. *(Looks at FANNY)* We're going to take up the scenes as they come along. Now—we're set on the prologue.

BERNIE Right. }
MAC O K.   } *(Together)*

LEHMAN How about you, Benham—prologue O.K.?

BENHAM *(Angry)* Oh, I am quite satisfied. *(Turns chair L)*

LEHMAN Well, don't get sore about it. Make a note—Prologue O.K.

PETER *(Up R C.)* O.K. (ALL *look at him*)

MARTIN *(In chair L.)* May I say something?

LEHMAN *(To MARTIN)* What is it?

MARTIN *(Rises; crosses to c)* The trouble with your play is that the leading character doesn't have sympathy. I'm fighting the audience all the time. I feel it. They don't like me.

FANNY *(Rises slowly)* Well, I think you were fine. I really do. *(Sits slowly)* That'll give you a rough idea of *my* condition. *(Settles self in chair)*

MARTIN *(Furious tapping of toe, trying to control herself)* Really, Mr. Lehman, if I'm to be required——

LEHMAN Shut up, Fanny! *(To MARTIN)* What is it?

MARTIN *(A little L of bed)* I'm *trying* to tell you that I'm not getting sympathy Something ought to be put in to show that I'm really all right at heart

PEGGY. *(On lower end of bed)* How about giving out pamphlets?

BERNIE Hey! Baby!

MARTIN. *(A glare at PEGGY, then turns to LEHMAN again)* If I could have a scene early in the play that would show me in a more sympathetic light —say a scene with a baby.

LEHMAN. We'll come back to it *(To JANE)* Make a note. Sympathy for Miss Martin.

PETER. If it's early in the play, Mr. Lehman, it can't be a baby, because she isn't married then.

LEHMAN All right. *(Loud knock by WAITER off U L.) All right* See who that is. *(PETER goes up)* Now we're going ahead from the prologue. *(PETER opens the door. The WAITER enters with food, crossing around bed to up R C)*

PEGGY. *(As WAITER passes bed)* Ah! The troops!

BERNIE. *(WAITER puts container up R and passes sandwich to PEGGY; she is the only one he passes any to; puts tray on chiffonier)* Sssh!

LEHMAN *(With emphasis, rises)* We are going

ahead from the prologue. The next is the orchard scene.

PETER. *(Crossing to* LEHMAN*)* I want to say something about that, Mr. Lehman.

LEHMAN. *(At* C *)* You don't tell me!

PETER Yes, sir. I was just waiting till you reached it. You see——

LEHMAN. Would you mind letting *me* talk for a minute?

PETER No, sir.

LEHMAN Much obliged. *(To* JANE*)* Give me that stuff. (PETER *gets over back of* LEHMAN. KITTY HUMPHREYS, *a pretty switchboard girl, enters up* L. *from* L *)*

MAC (KITTY *crosses down to* MAC *on his* R *at* L C *)* Oh, here's Kitty, Joe!

LEHMAN What? *(Sits back of table again)*

MAC. Here's Kitty from the switchboard.

LEHMAN. Oh!

MAC. Come on, Kitty.

FANNY Now we're going to get the real low-down. (WAITER *looks at* FANNY.*)*

MAC This is Miss Humphreys, everybody. Kitty, here's the angle. We want you to tell us just what you think of the show tonight, see? Straight from the shoulder. Now, you see all the shows that come here. We want to know your real opinion. (PEGGY, *on bed, eyes* KITTY *angrily)*

KITTY Well, I'll tell you, Jack—er—Mr. Mc-Clure You see, Syracuse is a funny town.

FANNY Oh, *that's* it?

KITTY *(To the people on her* R *)* It's a hard town to please, sort of—because you see we get *all* the new shows The managers all bring their shows here, because they know if it goes *here*, it'll go *any* place. You see, the people here are funny, sort of If they *like* a show they'll *go* to it, but if they don't like it—they *won't!*

LEHMAN. Well, that's a hot lot of news

WAITER. *(Crosses to* L. *of* LEHMAN*)* Excuse me. I can tell you what's wrong with your show. I wasn't there, but the chambermaid on Number four——

LEHMAN. *(Rises and yells)* Mac——Mac——— *(*PEGGY *rises and crosses to tray up* R C *)*

MAC. Just a minute. We want this young lady to—— *(*WAITER *looks at* MAC *)*

WAITER Oh, I beg your pardon. *(Back up* C *a few steps* PEGGY *crosses to* C *)*

KITTY. Well——

PEGGY. *(Crosses* C *to direct front of* KITTY*)* Are you the operator that took——

BERNIE *(Gets off of bed, crosses to* PEGGY *at her* R *)* Baby——

PEGGY. A New York call out of four thirteen this evening?

BERNIE. Now, baby——

PEGGY. Are you?

KITTY I may have been.

BERNIE Now don't——

MAC Now— } *(In unison)*

LEHMAN Say——

PEGGY. You were pretty fresh, weren't you?

KITTY I don't think so.

MAC Kitty——

PEGGY Well, I do——

BERNIE. Now—now——

PEGGY. And if you ever try it on me again——

LEHMAN. Get them out of here, will you?

MAC. Now listen, girls—— }

PEGGY Are you or are you not } *(In unison)* supposed to be respectful?

BERNIE Now, baby——

KITTY I'm always respectful, madam, when I'm speaking to a lady.

PEGGY. *(Very calmly)* I'll push your god-damn face in!

BERNIE. Baby—— *(Grabs* PEGGY. MAC *grabs*
KITTY *and swings her upstage in front of him, holding her by the arm)*

LEHMAN Get her out, Mac.

FANNY. Hurrah—— (MAC *takes*
KITTY *up* L.*)*

KITTY. (MAC *and* KITTY *stop up*
L.*)* You know where you can find me.   *(Together)*

PEGGY. *(Up at head of bed on* R
side) I can guess. (KITTY *exits up* L
PEGGY *sits on bed and fixes pillow behind her back, she eyes* LEHMAN)

BERNIE Now stop it.

LEHMAN Stop—everybody *(Crosses to* L *and
back to table)* How are we going to get anything
decided with all this—a-a-ah! *(Sits back of table
R.C)*

FANNY. I vote we make this a permanent or-
ganization and meet once a week.

LEHMAN We're here to decide about this show.

WAITER. *(Crosses down to* LEHMAN *on his* L *)*
I was going to tell you what this chambermaid said—

LEHMAN I don't want to know! Get out !

WAITER Yes, sir *(Crosses to* L *of bed)* Here's
the check. *(Looks at* PETER.*)*

PETER. *(Down, takes it, pays it)* Gosh !

LEHMAN. Where were we? (BERNIE *sits on
bed.)*

MAC. You were up to the prologue

PETER All right. *(Pays* WAITER *)*

WAITER Much obliged. *(Exits up* L *)*

LEHMAN. All right Now—the orchard scene.

PETER The trees aren't planted right

MAC Take it easy, Joe

LEHMAN Oh, they ain't, huh?

PETER No, sir. In a real orchard——

LEHMAN *(Rises)* Now, listen I'm pretty near
fed up—get me? You been interrupting all night—

one fool idea after another—and I had all I can stand.

PETER   But—but this isn't a—fool idea I'm right about it.

LEHMAN. All right, and I tell you I don't want to hear about it. Who's producing this show, anyhow?

PETER   Well, I'm part producer of it, and——

LEHMAN. (BERNIE *rises and watches scene*) Yah? Well, I'm the main producer Get me? And I'm going to do the talking! Forty-nine per cent—that's what you got

PETER   Well—I didn't mean to—do anything, but —you told me to take notes, and——

LEHMAN   You're going to keep on, are you?

PETER. No, sir, but if I see something I know is wrong. An orchard isn't planted that way The trees——

LEHMAN   *(Exasperated beyond control)* Good gawd! You half-wrecked the show, prowling around back stage, and then come here and—— What in blazes do you know about show business? I been all my life in it and you come green out of the country trying to tell me—— *I'm* running this show—you're nothing but a butter-and-egg man. Now, keep still! *(Crosses back to table; sits.)*

MAC. *(Pacifying)* Now, this ain't no way——

PETER. *(Turns to* MAC *at* C.) What—what did he say I was?

LEHMAN   Never mind! Only I want you to butt out of this show, see? I had all I can stand, and I want you to keep out!

JANE *(Rises, stands at table)* Mr Lehman, that isn't fair He hasn't done half as much as the others (PETER *back to audience)*

LEHMAN   Oh—— *(Fast and mean)* Now it's your business, is it?

JANE. I simply say you're being unfair to him.

I think—I think it's an outrageous way to treat him
You take his money—all you can get—for a play
you must have known was worthless——

LEHMAN. *(Rises)* Oh, I did, eh! And who asked
you to say anything? Huh?

JANE. I've stayed silent as long as I can.

LEHMAN. Then suppose you get the hell out of
here—and you needn't come back.

PETER   Hold on, there ⌐

JANE. Peter!   ⎱
LEHMAN   What?⎰   *(Together)*

PETER   This is *my* room. You can't order her
out.

LEHMAN   I can't, eh? *(Crosses D. one step.)*

PETER   No, sir. I mean *no*

LEHMAN   I warn you to lay off me.

PETER   Well—well, I won't   You—you can't talk
to her like that here—or any other place.

LEHMAN. I'll talk to her any way I want to—and
you too.

PETER. Well, you won't   Because—I won't let
you. *(Crosses up to bed and down C again)*

LEHMAN. Oh ⌐ Besides running the show you're
going to run me? Go on back to your sap town,
whatever it was   And you can take her with you,
because she's fired.

PETER   She wouldn't work for you anyhow, any
longer   Do you want to know why?

LEHMAN. I'd love to.

PETER. *(At C)* Because she's going to work for
me. You think I don't know anything, huh? I'm
just a bread-and-butter man? *(Looks L , then to
LEHMAN)* And I don't know anything about shows,
huh? *(Crosses up C. a little)*

LEHMAN. How'd you guess it?

PETER   *(Crosses to LEHMAN)* Well, I'll show
you whether I know anything about them   And I'll
show you whether you can talk to people like that.

Do you want to sell the rest of it—to me—the show?
(MARTIN *rises*)

JANE   Peter, you can't

PETER   *(L. of* MAC*)* Do you?

LEHMAN   *(Pauses   Crosses around* PETER *to*
MAC, L C. *Pauses   To* PETER, *who is L. of table*
R C *)* I might, for a price. It's a valuable property.

PETER   How much?

LEHMAN. What do you say, Mac?

MAC. Up to you, Joe.

LEHMAN   McClure and me is in together. Give
us—ten thousand apiece and the show's yours.
(JANE *touches* PETER'S *arm not to do it*)

PETER   I'll give you five thousand apiece.

LEHMAN   Seventy-five hundred

PETER. Five thousand.

LEHMAN   Cash?

PETER   *(Takes money from pants pocket, looks
down at it, not at them)* You give me—an option—
'til this time tomorrow—and I'll give you—five hundred dollars for it. It's about all I have—with me.

JANE   Peter, you can't.

PETER   You're all witnesses   *(Looks up)*

LEHMAN   Five thousand apiece for the rest of
the show   Ten thousand altogether

PETER. For Lehmac Productions—all of it

LEHMAN   And a one-day option. That goes
(Crosses to PETER *for money)* Give me the five hundred

PEGGY   Thank God ! That's settled   (PETER *gives
money to* LEHMAN *and he puts it in pocket   Then*
LEHMAN *and* MAC *shake hands)*

PETER. You all know the arrangement

FANNY   I'm a witness   *(Gets up, takes glass, but
leaves bottle)*

LEHMAN   *(Picks up coat off foot of bed)* Well,
I guess that's that   *(Puts on coat, takes out cigar)*

PEGGY   Can we go now? *(Rises, putting on hat, looking in mirror at R.)*

MARTIN. *(Sweetly At L)* Well, Mr. Jones——

PETER. Now, if you all wouldn't mind leaving—

PEGGY. (BERNIE *helps her put coat on)* Mind—did he say?

LEHMAN. I wish you luck and I hope you take up the option. *(Starts out, cigar in mouth.)*

PETER. I'll take it up

LEHMAN Coming, Fanny? *(As he crosses up L.C.)*

FANNY. Ya. *(Puts glass of wine on serving-tray up R.C.)*

MAC. Good night, Mr Jones—you know me *(Crossing out.)*

PETER. Yah (LEHMAN *exits up L.* MAC *exits up L after* LEHMAN.)

BENHAM *(At L C)* Will you require my services, Mr Jones? (PEGGY *crosses in front of* BENHAM *to up L.C.)*

PETER I'll let you know tomorrow

BENHAM *(Bows and turns up L , gets hat off bed)* Thanks

PEGGY *(Stops)* Well, it was a dandy trip *(Exits up L.)*

BENHAM *(Turns to* PETER, *hat in hand)* Good evening. *(Exits up L)*

PETER Good evening

BERNIE. *(A wave of the hand, crosses up L C)* Good luck to the show *(Stops up L)* All you need is to fix it *(Puts hat on and exits L.)*

MARTIN Don't forget Anything at all that you want to tell me *(Exits up L As* MARTIN *goes,* FANNY *crosses from R of bed to L of bed)*

FANNY Something tells me you haven't got the money

PETER. I'll get it—some place.

FANNY. Well—anyhow——— *(Exits up* L.; *shuts door)*

PETER   Well!

JANE.   Why did you do it? Why?

PETER. He just got me mad, I guess   *(Crosses up* L. *Crosses back io* JANE*)* What was that he said I was—about butter?

JANE.   Never mind

PETER.   Butter—a butter-and-egg man, that was it. What's that mean?

JANE.   It isn't anything

PETER.   It must mean something

JANE   It's—it's just a man that invests money, that's all   That puts money into something.

PETER.   Oh!

JANE   Peter, you must think what you're going to do. You gave him all your money, didn't you— that five hundred? Oh, Peter, it was foolish.

PETER. *(Crosses away and back)* I couldn't help it   I couldn't help it when he started talking to you like that

JANE   I got you into it again

(READY 'Phone)

PETER   Oh, no¹ You didn't   I mean, I'm glad you did. I mean I'm glad I feel that way about you. I know why you thought I was going to hate you. Because the play wasn't good   As if I could

JANE.   But, Peter, where are you going to get the money? Ten thousand dollars.

PETER   He—he got me so mad I thought sure I could get it some place   *(Turns and looks front)*

JANE.   Do you know anyone here in Syracuse?

PETER   *(Shakes his head)* I don't know anyone anywhere, with—ten thousand dollars.

JANE   Think hard¹ Peter—is there anyone in Chillicothe?

PETER. *(Pauses, as the mention of Chillicothe reminds him)* I sent her a telegram just after the show, saying it was a big success. *(Looks at* JANE*)* My mother, I mean

JANE Peter! Now, it's going to be one yet!

PETER *(Shakes his head)* I—I'm just beginning to realize what's happened I gave him about everything I had left and—that's all there is to it. It's gone I guess I'm done for. *(Crosses up* R.C. *and to chair at table)*

JANE. Peter, you're not.

PETER. *(At table* R C *)* No It's gone, all right. And she expected me to do such big things—— I'm not ever going home again

JANE Peter! Don't say that!

PETER I was a fool—— *(Looks through scripts and piles them on* L. *side of table)* all right—thinking I knew anything about shows She was depending on me, too—and now look what I've done to her—— I'm going to kill—*(Sits)* myself

JANE. *(Crosses to him quickly)* Peter, don't talk like that ! You're breaking my heart I know things are going to be better I just *feel* that something is going to *happen* *('Phone rings once)* That may be something now—— *('Phone rings again)*

PETER *(Looks up at* JANE, *worried ; rises; 'phone rings again , he starts for 'phone and it rings until he reaches it At 'phone up* L *)* Hello Yah, this is Mr. Jones Why, no—there isn't any—— Oh, yes— there is. All right Right away *(Hangs up and places 'phone on table.)*

JANE. Well?

PETER. You're not allowed to stay here any longer. It's against the rules.

JANE. *(At* R *of bed)* Oh, well—we'll meet first thing in the morning and plan something then. Won't we? And you're not going to be unhappy? *(Crosses down to foot of bed)*

PETER No matter what happens, I met you.

JANE. If only you hadn't.

PETER *(Crosses D to foot of bed)* Oh, but I love you, Jane I do, terribly And if ever I get out of this trouble—don't you think—really——

JANE. Peter—I think you're just the finest person that ever lived But I've got you into an awful mess I didn't mean to but I have And that's why I can't——

PETER Well—— *(Crosses away to L)* I'll get out of it some way You just see if I don't I'll get the money some place and—the play—— *(Crosses back to her in front of bed)* It might be a success in New York, don't you think?

JANE. It—might.

PETER I mean—even if it isn't awfully good. That isn't supposed to matter so much in New York, is it?

JANE Oh, Peter, I'm afraid——

PETER It—it just *can't* be a failure, that's all. It just can't be I bet if they'd just wait till we got a little money some place. (OSCAR *knocks at door up* L. PETER *looks at* JANE OSCAR *counts seven, knocks again* PETER *turns to door)* Who's there?

OSCAR. (OSCAR FRITCHIE *is a sufficiently nice-looking young man, but just a little dumb)* This is Mr. Fritchie.

PETER Who?

OSCAR Mr. Fritchie The assistant manager

PETER *(Crosses to* JANE; JANE *crosses a couple of steps to* PETER*)* He's the man that got us the champagne. *(A couple of steps to door)* What do you want?

OSCAR Can I come in? (PETER *looks at* JANE; *she nods "yes"* PETER *crosses up and opens door* OSCAR *enters up* L)

PETER. The door wasn't locked.

JANE. I was just leaving.

OSCAR. *(Up* L.C) Huh? Oh, broke up early, eh?

PETER. *(At door)* This is—Mr Fritchie, Miss Weston.

JANE. How are you?

OSCAR. Hello.

PETER Miss Weston was just going out when you —she was just going out—— *(Crosses down to* OSCAR *on his* L *)*

OSCAR. Oh Well, don't let me disturb you I just——

PETER. Isn't that what you came about?

OSCAR Huh?

PETER. They just telephoned me from downstairs —on account of Miss Weston being here.

OSCAR. Oh, that's all right. They didn't know you were friends of mine *(Crosses* R C.)

PETER Thank you very much, Mr Fritchie. Is there something—*(Crosses to* C *after* OSCAR*)* we can do for you?

OSCAR. *(At* C *)* Oh, no, no—no I just—*(Turns to* PETER*)* how was everything, all right—the supper?

PETER. Oh, yes Fine, thanks.

OSCAR And the champagne—did you get it all right?

PETER Yes. Thanks

OSCAR. You see, we get show troupes right along, up here, and—I know they got the habit of getting together, sort of—and—I like to—do whatever I can.

PETER That's fine—thanks, Mr. Fritchie

OSCAR. *(Crosses to table* R.C., *the same table* LEHMAN *used)* I—I'm kind of sorry your party's broken up.

JANE Yes. We are, too

OSCAR *(At* R C *)* I've always a kind of a liking for theatrical people, and of course, they stop here at the hotel a lot—and some of them sort of let me

come around   *(A couple of steps toward them)*
Just talk

PETER.   *(Turns to* JANE*)* Why, sure—we—*huh?*

JANE   Why—yes.

PETER.   Yes.

OSCAR.   Louis Mann was here last year.   *(Hands in pockets)* We had quite a *long talk*

PETER.   Well, we don't mind talking at all—if—
Is there something special you want to talk about?

OSCAR   *(Crosses back of table* R.C.*)* Oh, no—no
—nothing in particular.   You know how it is——
(Turns to them) You get a liking for something—
the theatre—— All my life I've—I've just kind of
liked to talk about it, that's all   I guess maybe it's
because I've always had a sort of feeling that some
day I might get into it— *(Puts hands in pockets)*
myself   (OSCAR *looks front*   PETER *has hand to
head during this speech.)*

PETER   *(Takes hand from head, crosses a little to
C.   Long pause)* Would you mind saying that
again?

OSCAR   The show business   I say—some day I'm
going to get into it

PETER   *(A couple of steps to* OSCAR*)* You don't
mean—as a producer?

OSCAR   *(Pleased, looks front)* That's what
(Pause PETER *looks at* JANE, *looks at* OSCAR, *shakes
his head, crosses up, crosses down, looks at* JANE *)*

PETER.   Sit down, Sweetheart   *(Places chair back
of* OSCAR, *then crosses up* L.*)*

OSCAR.   Who, me?   *(Puzzled*   PETER *nods)* I
don't mean to butt in   I just——

PETER   *(Crosses to back of table* R C.*)* That's all
right

OSCAR   Well—much obliged   *(Sits)*

JANE   *(Crosses to* L *of table)* You—you said
you were the assistant manager?

OSCAR.   Yah   Mr. Hemingway is the manager

PETER   *(Crosses to* R. *of table)* I used to work
in a hotel, before I went into the theatre business

OSCAR. That so?

PETER   *(Hand on back of chair* R *of table)* That
must be a fine job you have here. You must make a
lot of money?

OSCAR   Oh, I don't suppose you folks would call
it much

JANE. Oh, yes, we would.

PETER   Look, Mr. Fritchie. Have you—that is,
have you been able to—in all this—have you got any
saved up—I mean money?

OSCAR. Huh?

JANE   Mr Jones has known so many hotel men
who didn't save He just hopes you're different.

OSCAR   That's right A lot of them don't

PETER   *(Bending over* OSCAR*)* I know But you
do, don't you? That's what we want to get down to

OSCAR   You bet your life I do.

PETER. That's fine. *(Turns* R.*)*

OSCAR   What's the matter?

JANE. Not a thing.

PETER. Nothing   *(Alone)* Would
you like a glass of champagne?   } *(Together)*
(Crosses up and gets it)

OSCAR. *(Still in chair)* Say—that's not a bad idea.
(Turns L *to* JANE*)* You know, I like you folks.
You make a fellow feel nice.

PETER   *(At* OSCAR'S R. *with glass of wine)* Here,
drink this first. *(Puts glass on table and stands by
dresser)*

OSCAR   Well, here's to you. *(Drinks.* PETER
salutes toast.)

JANE   *(As he finishes)* Some more? *(Crosses
up, gets champagne)*

OSCAR   I'm not robbing you?

PETER. No—no—it's all right. (JANE *crosses to*
R. *of* OSCAR; *pours champagne in same glass)*

OSCAR. Yes, sir—I always say show folk are nice people. Not stuck-up, you know—make a fellow feel at home. *(Finish pouring.)* Oh, thanks (PETER *puts bottle back up stage after* OSCAR *ends drink* PETER *crosses around and to* OSCAR, *at his* L)

PETER. *(Puts hand on* OSCAR'S *shoulder)* Er—

OSCAR Huh?

PETER *(Worried)* Nothing—yet. *(Crosses to* L. *of bed)*

OSCAR Say—what's going on here?

JANE. Mr. Jones has a proposition to make to you He's going to give you a chance to invest in this play that opened tonight It's going to make an awful lot of money——

OSCAR. Well, I don't want to invest *(Rises.)*

PETER *(Crosses to* OSCAR*)* Now wait! You didn't see the play tonight, did you?

OSCAR. No.

PETER That's fine. It's going to be much better. It's a big drama, see, with this girl in it and—and—do you know how much money a lot of shows have made?

OSCAR You bet your life I do "Madame Sherry" made seven hundred and fifty thousand dollars. "Potash and Perlmutter" made half a million. "Within the Law" made——

PETER. There you are ! Isn't that wonderful ?

JANE Mr Jones'll tell you what a wonderful play this is, Mr. Fritchie. And he has a chance to get hold of the whole thing—all of it It's a real chance —the chance of a lifetime.

PETER. Do you know what a brothel is ? Do you ?

OSCAR *(Looks at* JANE, *bashful)* Huh? Why— yes, I guess I do *(Sits)*

PETER Well, we've got one in this play and it's great, see? A priest and a rabbi come into it—it's a great big scene (OSCAR *looks at* PETER *)* It's going to be a knockout—everything happens to this girl—she marries a fellow and there's another fellow and she gets into a lot of trouble—only she's got to have more sympathy—so she's going to have a baby —it's going to make millions of dollars—thousands.

OSCAR *(Rises)* I don't think I want to——

PETER. Everything is changed around—it's going to have Hong Kong in it—in place of where the trial scene is now—it's going to be a hop joint in Hong Kong It's a wow, and he turns out to be her father—with a long beard on—that's where we bring in the strong talk and so and so, and so and so, and so and so That's your first act. *(Crosses over to foot of bed, taking off dress coat as he goes, throws coat on bed, crossing back to* OSCAR*)* Then we go on from there

OSCAR Now—now—you got to stop, if you want me to—— *(Considers)* Go into the theatrical business, eh? It would be fun.

PETER. Oh, it's an awful lot of fun—you haven't any idea.

OSCAR Would it cost much money?

PETER. No. You can have half of it—that is— forty-nine percent—for thirty thousand dollars *(Crosses away toward* C *)*

OSCAR. *(Crosses to* PETER *and* PETER *back to* L *)* Thirty thousand dollars!

PETER Twenty-five thousand!

OSCAR. Twenty-five thousand?

PETER. Twenty! Fifteen!

JANE. And that's—— *(Slaps table)* the very lowest, Mr. Fritchie!

OSCAR *(Crosses to table; sits)* It's a lot.

JANE. Oh, no, it's a bargain.

PETER *(Reads fast)* Yes. Only you have to decide quickly—because the man that decides right away—I mean *standing up*—— *(Motions up with hands.* OSCAR *rises slowly)* You see, Mr. Fritchie,

everything in the show business is done like that——
(Makes a poor attempt at snapping fingers) We
read about a fellow who could have bought some of
the "Follies" once, only he didn't—and look, it's all
gone now

OSCAR. Now, wait. I—I don't know what to say.
I know I'd like the theatrical business, and I been—
(Looks front) getting kind of tired of the hotel
lately——

PETER. Of course you would. You're not the kind
of man to stay cooped up in a hotel all his life

JANE Mr Jones got out, and look at him.

PETER *(Backs away toward C. a couple of steps)*
Yes. Look at me.

JANE It's going to make an awful lot of money

OSCAR *(Looks front)* I'd love to quit and tell
Mr. Hemingway what I thought of him.

PETER *(Crosses to OSCAR)* That's the stuff!

JANE. Then why don't you?

OSCAR. I'm scared

PETER. Well, this is your chance.

JANE. A chance to leave this old hotel behind you.

PETER. I guess—— *(Crosses away to L again)*
when he looks back at an opportunity he's missed,
like this, it will make him feel pretty terrible When
it's a big success in New York——

OSCAR. *(Crosses to PETER C)* Now—now wait
I haven't said I wouldn't, yet.

PETER. You've got to act quick with us, if you
want it.

OSCAR You say it's—a good play?

PETER *(At L C.)* Good! There's never been anything like it

OSCAR *(At C)* There are certainly some things
I'd tell Mr. Hemingway, the big stiff.

PETER *(Crosses to JANE at R quickly)* Make out
a receipt, Jane. (JANE *picks up pad and crosses to
dresser* R *quickly. Starts writing receipt)*

OSCAR. *(Crosses back of table)* Now, wait.

PETER *(At R of table)* No, unless you can give us your check right away, we can't do it at all   Can you?

OSCAR I haven't said I was going to at all, yet.

JANE. *(Play very fast. Turns to* OSCAR *from dresser)* But if you do it right away, you can go to Mr. Hemingway tonight and tell him all those things. Just *think   (Continues writing receipt.)*

OSCAR   *(Behind table R C)* He made me work twelve hours a day.

PETER. You don't have to work at all in the theatre.

OSCAR. He'd be sore, all right.

PETER   There's no reason why we have to produce just this one show. We could go ahead and do a lot more.

OSCAR   *(Takes out checkbook from inside coat pocket and stands with it in his hands, undecided)* Could we?

PETER Of course—couldn't we?

JANE Of course.

PETER. *(At R. of table)* Why, we can be the biggest producers there are   All kinds of shows——— Can I open that for you? *(Starts to open   OSCAR scans checkbook.)*

OSCAR *(Sits at table)* No. No.

PETER. *(At* OSCAR'S R)* Well, here is ink and pen and everything   You just make the check out to me—Peter Jones

(WARN Curtain)

JANE. What's your first name, Mr. Fritchie, and how do you spell this one?

OSCAR Oscar Fritchie   F-r-i-t-c-h-i-e

PETER *(Crosses to* JANE*)* F-r-i-t-c-h-i-e   Got it?

OSCAR. *(Continues as* PETER *spells name)* But I haven't made up my mind yet.

PETER. How are you coming here? Have you started yet?

OSCAR I don't know. You got me all excited—but——

JANE *(Reads fast)* Here's the receipt *(Crosses to R of table, puts the receipt on it)* It just says you're giving us the money for forty-nine per cent of it. *(Crosses to L of OSCAR)* Is that all right?

PETER. That's fine. Here's the receipt Now all you have to do is to sign the check, see? Here, I'll help you Oscar, it should be——

OSCAR *(As PETER starts to help him, OSCAR stops)* Do you think I ought to?

PETER. Of course you ought to It's a great big drama, and there's an orchard in it, and Mr Hemingway comes in, and he's got a long beard on Oh! Did I tell him about the bookings yet? Did I? We go from here to Providence, then Albany, and Seattle——

OSCAR Look out—— *(Tears out check and PETER grabs it)* It's wet

PETER I'll dry it *(Ring curtain)* It's going to be a whale of a hit. Sweetheart, a whale of a hit *(As curtains falls, OSCAR mops his head with handkerchief and JANE shakes his hand. PETER ad lib. as curtain falls.)*

CURTAIN

ACT III

SCENE: *Same as Act I; a few weeks later All that is missing is the overwhelming pile of papers that had stood against the rear wall.*

JANE *(Is seated at the desk at rise, looking over newspaper notices. 'Phone rings as curtain is up, it is out of her reach; she gets up to answer it)* Hello—— No, Mr. Jones hasn't come in yet—— Well, if you try a little later—— Yes, it looks like a very big hit At least, they seem to think so at the theatre, but of course it's a little early to tell—— Good-bye *(There is a knock at R She hangs up)* Come in! *(Crosses C, but the door is opened before she reaches it It is A J PATTERSON who enters, with brief case)*

PATTERSON *(Is a middle-aged business man, rather formidable in manner Crosses R.C after a quick look around the office)* Pardon me *(Takes hat off)* Mr. Jones is not in?

JANE No, sir—he isn't. Is there anything I can do for you?

PATTERSON His partner is not here either?

JANE Mr Fritchie? No I'm expecting them any minute

PATTERSON *(Considers, nods)* I'll return

JANE. Isn't there any message? Can't I give them your name?

PATTERSON *(Turns as he is about to go out)* Oh, this new play of theirs—I understand that it's successful Is that right?

JANE Yes, sir—I think so. But of course it only opened last night.

PATTERSON. I see. Thank you. *(Turns to go; puts hat on.)*

JANE You—you still won't tell me who it is?

PATTERSON. *(Left hand on doorknob, turns back)* You needn't worry. I shall return *(He goes out at R)*

(JANE, impressed by his manner and a little worried, stands for a second looking at the closed door, then turns back to the desk. She has just taken up a newspaper again when PETER enters C., derby on, cigarette in holder-case, dark street suit.)

PETER *(Enters snappily)* Well! *(Crosses C , smiling, takes hat off.)*

JANE *(Crosses below desk to R of it)* Peter!

PETER *(Pleased)* Well, I guess I was right, wasn't I?

JANE What?

PETER The play's a hit Remember—— *(Crosses to hat tree up R C., just puts cane on it)* I told you it would be, when it came to New York? *(Crosses back to her)*

JANE Yes, Peter! I can hardly believe it People are lined up over at the theatre, buying tickets. Isn't it wonderful?

PETER. Oh, I don't know It wasn't any surprise to me *(Crosses to L of desk)* Is there any mail? *(Puts hat on desk and starts piling up newspapers on C part of desk)*

JANE. Ah—why, no Some people have been telephoning, and there was a gentleman here just now, but he wouldn't leave his name

PETER *(Business-like)* Did he state his business?

JANE No, he didn't

PETER Always ask them to state their business And—ah—if anybody else comes, bring in their cards first, please, to see if I'll see them. *(At* c. *of desk, looks at papers.)*

JANE   All right.

PETER.   You see, Jane, the reason you mustn't ever be surprised at a play like this being a hit is because it's so full of heart interest—*that's* what the public wants—*heart* interest—and *menace.* The moment I first heard of this play I knew it would be a success   *(Picks up newspapers again and holds them in his hands.)*

JANE.   *(Crosses to desk)*   I'm terribly happy, Peter, that you were right.

PETER   It doesn't amount to anything, once you learn how. Probably all of my productions will be successes now. *(He starts reading through two or three different papers.)*

JANE   That would be nice.

PETER.   *(Looks at* JANE*)*   Did you read these—the criticisms?   *(Pointing to criticism in paper)*

JANE.   Yes.

PETER   This fellow missed the whole idea of the play   *(Stands and puffs cigarette)*   And he thought the performance was only adequate   A lot they know about it—the critics   I'm thinking of not letting them come at *all* the next time. *('Phone rings. Picks ('PHONE)*

it up quickly)   Hello—— Yes, this is Mr. Jones speaking.—— Thank you—— Yeh, I guess it's about the biggest that's ever been produced—— Huh? *(Sits on desk)*   Oh, no—— I'm going to produce it *myself* in London. Budapest, too—— Yeh—a sort of international producing company. —Well, it wouldn't be any use of your coming over, because when I make up my mind I'm like that   Good-bye. *(Hangs up   Rises from desk)*   I'm going to produce it all over the world

JANE.   Do you want anything more from me now? *(Starts* R.*)*

PETER   *(Crosses front of desk to* JANE*)*   What's that matter, Jane?

JANE.   *(Crossing to* R *)*   Nothing

PETER.   Aren't you glad the play's a success?

JANE.   Of course   I'm very happy for you   I wish you just all the success in the world.   *(Back turned to him.)*

PETER   *(Crosses to her)*   It means an awful lot to us, Jane.

JANE.   *(Turns to him. Eagerly)*   Does it, Peter?

PETER   *(At* C.*)*   Oh! I forgot to tell you about a man I met this morning   He wants to build a theatre for me—the Peter Jones Playhouse

JANE.   I'll hardly know you, will I?

PETER.   *(Just* R *of* C. *door at* C.*)*   Jane, what would you say to changing the name of the firm, now that they're out of it?   Don't you think it would be simpler to have it just Jones Productions, Inc?

JANE   Yes, I suppose it would be simpler

PETER   Do you think—do you think my picture would make a good trademark?

JANE   If you—want it.

PETER   And oh, Jane——   (OSCAR *enters* R. *Pauses, hat in hand)*   Well?

OSCAR   Good morning!

JANE   Good morning, Mr Fritchie

OSCAR   Good morning, Miss Weston!

PETER   How do you feel now?

OSCAR   What are all those people doing over at the theatre?

PETER   The play's a big success

OSCAR.   Who says so?

PETER   Everybody   We're nearly sold out for to-night

OSCAR.   Yes—who'll come tomorrow night?

PETER   *(Crosses up, then to* L *of desk)*   Wait till you hear all the plans I've got.   Get Jane here to tell you about the Peter Jones Playhouse. *(Throws papers in waste-basket)*

JANE   I—I think there's someone in the outer office. *(Crosses to door R. in front of OSCAR.)*

PETER. Well, don't forget about bringing in their cards *(Sits at desk)*

JANE. *(In door)* I won't. *(Exits R., closing door.)*

OSCAR. *(Crosses to desk)* Now on the level, how are things?

PETER *(Smokes cigarette in holder)* It's one of the biggest successes ever produced.

OSCAR. *(Leans over desk)* She's gone—you can tell me.

PETER. People are calling up to buy it for London and every place.

OSCAR. *(Over desk, speaks quickly)* How much did you get?

PETER   I wouldn't sell it

OSCAR   Now look—I think if we can get *any* money we ought to, because—I don't feel just right yet, see? *(Turns away.)*

PETER   When we go ahead and produce the Peter Jones "Follies" you'll feel right

OSCAR   *(Turns back)* Do you think we ought to do that?

PETER. And this afternoon I'm seeing a man about the Hippodrome *(Smokes)*

OSCAR   I think——   *(Crosses to C.)* maybe I ought to get out *(Picks up hat from table)*

PETER   *(Puts cigarette down, picks up pen and receipt book)* All right   I can handle it myself.

OSCAR. *(Crosses back to desk quickly)* Would you be willing to buy my share back?

PETER. *(Opens receipt book as if to write)* You bet I would

OSCAR. Well—then I don't know. *(Crosses away a couple of steps)*

PETER. *(Rises, crosses to* OSCAR C *)* Do you know what I'm going to do if you stay with me? I'm going to get all the playwrights there are in this country, and put them under contract, and then we'll tie up all the foreign plays

OSCAR But suppose something happens?

PETER What can happen in the theatrical business? *(Puts cigarette on tray on desk)* Now, look! When we've got all the plays tied up, then the thing to do is to get all the theatres

OSCAR You don't think it could go wrong some place?

PETER. No You can't make a mistake—all you got to do is to give the public what they want

OSCAR Yah, but—but—but how do you know what they *want?*

PETER It's easy They always want the same thing

OSCAR *(Shakes his head)* Sure as I went into it they'd change their minds.

PETER We'll put another—(JANE *enters* R *with a card)*—company in Chicago—— *(Sees* JANE, *crosses to her in front of* OSCAR*)* See? A card! People are starting to come in already.

JANE It's the gentleman who was here before

PETER Yah? I've never heard of him *(Crosses to* OSCAR*)* Did you?

OSCAR *(At* R C, *looking at card, shakes head)* No And I don't know *why,* but I've got a feeling it's *bad* news.

PETER *(Reading card)* A J Patterson.

OSCAR *(Also reading)* Attorney-at-law *(Quickly)* That's the part I don't like *(Takes step* L *)*

PETER Did he say what he wanted?

JANE No, he didn't

PETER *(To* OSCAR*)* Oh, well, he's probably just come to make an offer Huh?

OSCAR   No—they don't make offers, attorneys-at-law.

PETER. You're getting me nervous now

OSCAR. I bet we've got the show in the wrong theatre

PETER *(To* JANE*)* Will you tell him to come in?

JANE Yes, sir *(Crosses to door, opens and holds it open)* Will you please come in, Mr Patterson? *(He enters and she closes door and stands with back to same PATTERSON enters* R *, comes in a few steps and holds.)*

PETER. Did you want to see me?

PATTERSON. *(Looks at* OSCAR*)* Which is Mr. Peter Jones?

OSCAR *(Sidesteps a little to the* L.*)* He is.

PATTERSON Is this Mr Oscar Fritchie?

OSCAR. Yep

PATTERSON I called on you gentlemen earlier and left word that I would return

OSCAR Yah? I—wish I'd known *(Another step* L.*)*

PATTERSON You have my card?

PETER Yes

PATTERSON My name is Patterson.

PETER *(Looks at card)* That's right.

PATTERSON I'm an attorney-at-law

OSCAR A lawyer, huh? *(Steps toward* PATTERSON.*)*

PATTERSON. *(Sternly)* An attorney-at-law.

OSCAR *(Turns and steps away to* L *one or two steps)* Oh!

PETER. Is there something we can do for you, Mr. Patterson?

PATTERSON. There is   May I—— *(Indicates desk* L C *)*

PETER *(*JANE *steps down below door* R *and holds)* Yes. Surely

(PATTERSON *crosses to upper end of desk, puts on glasses, takes documents from case, magazine, arranges them Long pause.* PETER *and* OSCAR *look at* PATTERSON, *then each other, worried* PATTERSON *clears throat, looks at legal paper*)

PATTERSON. You are the owners of Lehmac Productions, Incorporated, Fourteen Hundred and Sixty-eight Broadway, New York, New York. A New York corporation *(Looks at* PETER *)*

PETER We are *(Raises* R *hand)*

OSCAR He owns most of it *(Indicates* PETER *)*

PATTERSON *(Crossing* L *)* Said corporation being the producers of a dramatic composition or play, entitled "Her Lesson"

PETER Is it s-something about the play ? *(Crosses to* PATTERSON *in front of* OSCAR *)*

PATTERSON *(Back of desk)* In November, Nineteen—— *(Picks up magazine, reads year and date from magazine)* Hundred and Sixteen there appeared in this magazine, "Peppy Tales," published in New York City, an article of fiction, or short story, entitled "A Woman's Honor" Said story— *(Crosses to* L *)* having been written by my client, Mr. Rodney Rich, of Northampton, Massachusetts— *(Crosses back to desk)* and, as we shall duly prove in court——

OSCAR In court?

PATTERSON *(Puts magazine on desk and again picks up legal paper)* In court

OSCAR. I thought you said court

PATTERSON The said story was, on— *(Reads from legal paper)* January Eight, Nineteen Hundred and Seventeen, accepted as the basis of a play by one Harley Thompson, since deceased

PETER *(*OSCAR *looks to* PETER *to explain)* Dead

PATTERSON Subsequently, as we shall prove, the said play was purchased, or acquired, by one Joseph

Lehman— (PETER *looks at* OSCAR) and by him duly produced. It will be shown that the said dramatic composition, or play, is similar to the aforesaid short story at—*(Looks at legal paper again)* one hundred and forty-six points.

PETER. One hundred and forty-*six*? *(Turns to* PATTERSON *again)*

PATTERSON And that no less than *six* characters in the aforesaid play bear the same names as those in the aforesaid short story. *(Looks at* PETER *)*

PETER *(A few steps to* PATTERSON*)* Well, was the aforesaid——?

PATTERSON. One moment, please. *(Crosses down on* R. *side of desk)* My client, Mr Rodney Rich, has received no payment for this play, nor has his permission been sought in any way *(Stops at lower end of desk)* It is, gentlemen, a clear case of plagiarism— *(Crossing up on* L *side of desk)* and one of the most flagrant that it has *ever* been my privilege to encounter *(Arrives again at upper end of desk)*

OSCAR. But—but—but—look here——

PETER We didn't know anything about it. I bought it from Mr Lehman, and then Mr. Fritchie here——

PATTERSON Unfortunately—— *(Looks at legal papers again)*

OSCAR. That's a *bad* word

PATTERSON *(At upper end of desk)* My client cannot take that matter into account. His composition has been produced in dramatic form without his consent. Not unnaturally he seeks redress

OSCAR. Seeks what?

PATTERSON *(*OSCAR *looks at* PETER *for him to explain)* Redress.

PETER Money

PATTERSON My purpose in placing these facts before you, prior to bringing suit—is to afford you the opportunity,—if you so desire, of adjusting the

matter outside of court *(Places legal paper on desk.
Oscar indicates Peter to do something)*

PETER   Well—well—what are we supposed to do?
(Crosses a couple of steps to Patterson)

PATTERSON. My client will accept sixty-six and
two-thirds per centum of all profits derived from
said play, when, if and as produced, and in those
circumstances will permit the play to continue Fail-
ing to receive sixty-six and two-thirds per centum—

OSCAR   *(Nods head to Peter)* That's money,
too

PATTERSON   He will apply for an injunction and
cause the play to be closed at once

PETER   He'll close it?

PATTERSON   He will close it.

OSCAR   Close it?

PATTERSON   *(Very firm and fierce)* You understand me. *(Turns and puts magazine and papers in
case and shuts it, puts glasses in pocket.)*

OSCAR   Yah. Look Most of it's yours, see? I
don't know much about law, see? You—do something, and I'll go over and see if the theatre's burned
down yet *(Puts hat on, exits R , closing door)*

PETER. *(Crosses U R after Oscar's exit)* What
are we going to do?

JANE *(Crosses to C.)* Must Mr Jones give an
answer immediately?

PATTERSON   I regret that he must.

PETER *(Crosses down R C on Jane's R)* But—I
haven't had time——

JANE. *(At C)* Can't we—even talk it over? That
is, Mr Jones and I?

PATTERSON *(Crosses down to them R C)* This
young lady is your adviser?

PETER   Yes, indeed

PATTERSON *(Crosses R to door)* At best, I could
allow but a brief time *(Opens door)*

PETER   Well, that would be better than——

PATTERSON. *(In door)* Shall we say—fifteen minutes?

PETER. Shall we?

PATTERSON Very well. *(Puts on hat)* I shall return for your decision in fifteen minutes. *(Exits R , closing door)*

PETER Oh, Jane!

JANE Oh, Peter, you mustn't worry

PETER *(Crosses L to R side of desk)* Oh, Jane— just when everything was going along so fine, to have——

JANE *(At C)* But you mustn't get discouraged He—may not be right at all

PETER *(At lower end of desk, his back to her)* Oh, yes, he is. I remember Mr Lehman said something about its being a story, that very first day

JANE *(Crosses to PETER at his R.)* But this may not be it Now, when he comes back we'll make him show all his proofs——

PETER. It's no use, Jane—— Sixty-six and two-thirds per centum—— And I was going to do such big things *(Sits R. of desk)*

JANE. You will yet, Peter.

PETER. I guess I wasn't supposed to do them. Some people that sort of naturally do big things, and others that—like—— I wouldn't care if it weren't— *(Puts elbows on table, rests chin in hands)* for— everything.

JANE *(Pauses, backs away a step)* Peter—may I tell you something? I love you.

PETER *(Rises; crosses to her)* Do you?

JANE *(At C)* I wanted to tell it to you now, when things are—looking black. It—it may be wrong, but—I'm glad this has happened.

PETER *(Takes her hands)* Glad?

JANE Of course—I'm sorry about the money, but I'm awfully glad for you

PETER How do you—mean, Jane?

JANE I did want you to be successful, but some-how you lost something that was you It's just as you said, Peter—you're not that kind of person—you never could be You belong back in Chillicothe, in the hotel You're sweet and—simple and—you don't really like all this, do you ?

PETER I don't know I thought I did, but—I don't know *(Turns away, she still holds his* R *hand)*

JANE. Don't you see—how little it amounts to, really ? You're too fine for it, Peter.

PETER *(Turns to her)* Did you mean that, about —loving me ? *(Hands on her arms)*

JANE More than anything that ever was *(Head on his shoulder, pause)* I thought—— *(Raises head)* for a while you'd gone away from me, but now I know you never can It made me so unhappy to think that—but now it's all over

PETER *(Crosses to lower end of desk)* It's over, all right Being a success is all over.

JANE You mustn't mind

PETER I wanted it to go on account of you, and now there isn't anything and that lawyer'll be com-ing back and——

JANE But suppose you gave him what he wanted —what difference does it make ?

PETER I couldn't I hardly have a thing left Besides, I got Oscar to go into this and—— *(JANE crosses to* C *Knock on* C *door)* He wouldn't be here already, would he?

JANE *(Crosses up, opens* C *door)* Mrs. Leh-man.

FANNY Hello *(Enters up* C *)*

PETER *(At lower end of desk)* Oh—hello

FANNY *(Crosses to* C *)* Hello ! Well, you ought to be peppier than this Do you know you've got a hit ?

PETER *(At* FANNY'S L *)* Yes, ma'am

FANNY. Yes, sir—a hit. I don't know what that proves about the public, but it's certainly something

JANE *(Crosses down to* FANNY's R *)* You've come to tell us something.

FANNY You're pretty cute

JANE Well?

FANNY You've got company coming.

JANE. Mr. Lehman?

FANNY. Right.

JANE. Soon?

FANNY. On the fire

PETER. What's he want?

FANNY. He's smoked out a bankroll and he wants to buy back the show.

PETER. No?—Oh—— *(To* JANE*)* S-a-y—— *(Then* R. *and back down* R.C.*)* Look. You don't think he will get here pretty soon—*(Looking at watch)* in less than fifteen minutes, do you think?

FANNY What's going on?

PETER Do you?

FANNY. *(Nods)* I just shot ahead of him to tell you that he's picked up a little tip.

PETER. Huh? }
JANE. What is it? } *(Together)*

FANNY You know I got a kind of a fool liking for you two Somehow, suckers always did appeal to me.

PETER. You were going to tell us? He might get here, and——

FANNY. It's this You've got about three times as big a hit as you think you have.

PETER No!

FANNY You know that brothel scene?

PETER Yes, indeed

FANNY. The police are going to try to close the show. That means you'll be hanging 'em up on the rafters.

PETER   Gosh! *(LEHMAN knocks up C door Backs away)*

FANNY   Joe raised the money on that tip   He's got it on him in certified checks.

JANE   How much?

FANNY   I don't know. *(LEHMAN knocks again.)*

PETER   A butter-and-egg man. *(They hold till PETER sits at desk, and puts feet up   FANNY crosses to R   JANE crosses to up C door   PETER, hat on, feet upon desk a la LEHMAN   JANE opens C door   LEHMAN pauses, enters up C.)*

JANE   Good morning, Mr Lehman.

LEHMAN   *(To JANE)* Hi—— *(Looks at FANNY and comes C.)* Morning.

PETER.   *(Pauses, as LEHMAN gets down C)* How are you, Sweetheart?

LEHMAN.   *(To FANNY)* What are you doing here?

FANNY   Just visiting.

LEHMAN.   *(At C)* Get out!

JANE   *(Crosses down C on LEHMAN'S R)* I—I think Mrs. Lehman ought to stay.

PETER   You're not going to start putting people out of places again, are you? Now, let's all sit down and—visit   Unless there's something particular you want to say.

LEHMAN   I don't know what she's been handing you, but don't start in believing it. *(Hands in vest pockets)*

PETER   About what?

LEHMAN   We can skip all that. I came around to give you your coin back—and let you out clean

PETER   Oh, you mean you want to buy the show?

LEHMAN   *(At C.)* I'll give you what you paid for it—twenty and ten—thirty thousand   You won't lose a thing

PETER   *(Laughs)* You won't either, will you?

LEHMAN.   What?

PETER. The point is, it's a valuable property, see? It starts with a prologue and it's——

LEHMAN *(Crosses to upper end of desk)* You're going to believe that stuff of hers, huh? Listen, Sweetheart, I'm an old hand at this game—I can make something out of this show, but you can't.

PETER. The judge has got a long beard on.

LEHMAN I'll give you forty—and I've got the certified checks in my pocket Set? (JANE, *at* C, *shakes her head.* PETER *shakes his head*) Forty-five, and that's all That's netting you fifteen (JANE *shakes her head* PETER *shakes his head*) I only got fifty—— Do you want it all?

MAC *(Bursts in* C *door)* So—— *(To down* C *to* R. *of* JOE *and holds.* LEHMAN *looks around*)

FANNY The boy-friend *(All look at* FANNY.)

MAC. *(Swings door shut)* I thought so

LEHMAN. Thought what?

MAC. Trying to double-cross me? Eh? Have you sold it to him yet? *(Crosses down* R *of desk* LEHMAN *crosses to* C.R. *of* MAC.)

PETER. Why?

MAC. *(At* R *of desk)* If you haven't—don't— because he's going to skin you

PETER. Mr Lehman?

MAC. He didn't tell you about the police, did he?

FANNY. I did (ALL *look at* FANNY *again*)

LEHMAN Just a pal.

MAC Now listen I'll give you fifty thousand dollars. I've got it right here

PETER *(Rises, crosses to* LEHMAN) Fifty thousand? That's ridiculous Why, even Mr. Lehman offered that much.

MAC He did?

PETER Do you want to go any—*(Turns to* MAC) higher? It's a great play—there's a priest in it——

MAC. *(Turns to* LEHMAN) How about you, Mr. Lehman?

LEHMAN   *(Steps up* C *a little   To* FANNY*)* I'm going to brain you.

JANE.   I know a way to fix things   Mr. Lehman has fifty thousand dollars and so has Mr McClure

LEHMAN   *(Steps down again)* Well?

JANE   Why shouldn't they—buy it together?

PETER   *(Smiles)* Yah! That's an idea. Very good. *(Pats her on shoulder)* A hundred thousand dollars

LEHMAN.   What?

JANE   That's the price, Mr. Lehman.

LEHMAN   A hundred thousand?

PETER   Umhuh   *(*MAC *starts to sit)* And think on your feet   *(*MAC *rises* PETER *crosses to* L *of desk and sits, puts hat on desk)*

LEHMAN   *(Looking to* PETER *at desk)* That's final?

PETER   Yep.

FANNY   *(Crosses to filing cabinet near door* C *)* Five-Star.

PETER   *(Writing receipt)* Only I got to know right away   *(Snaps fingers)* That's the show game

LEHMAN   Come out here a minute, Mac.

MAC   O K   *(*MAC *exits first,* C *)*

LEHMAN.   *(To* PETER*)* We'll be right back *(Gives* FANNY *a look as he goes out* C *)*

PETER   Do   *(Rises   Crosses* C   JANE *on his* R. FANNY *crosses to his* L *)* You think they'll do it?

JANE   I think so   Oh, I hope so.   '

PETER   But suppose that lawyer comes back before they——

FANNY.   What lawyer?

PETER   Don't tell them, see—but there was a lawyer came in——   *(*OSCAR *knocks, enters* FANNY *crosses up to* C *door)*

PETER   There he is!   }
JANE   I'll keep him out here——   }   *(Together)*

OSCAR. (JANE *crosses up* C. *to* FANNY) Has he gone?

PETER *(Crosses* R. *to* OSCAR) Listen   Everything has changed, see? I haven't got time to tell you, but don't be nervous, and—and don't ask any questions.

OSCAR. Huh?

JANE. Don't say anything. *(Crosses down to* L *desk; sits.)*

OSCAR. What's going on? (LEHMAN *enters* C. *door and crosses down* C., MAC *on his* L *)* Look, look—— *(As they come down* C.*)* Hello.

MAC. Hello, how are you?

OSCAR   Not bad. My throat's a little bit——

PETER. *(To* LEHMAN*)* Have you—decided?

LEHMAN. Now look here a minute——

(KNOCK.)

(PATTERSON knocks off R 1.)

OSCAR   I'll go.

PETER *(Locks door and looks at watch)* No, no! It's—it's—— I know what it is, see? *(To* LEHMAN*)* You were going to say whether you'd decided.

OSCAR. But if there's somebody out there——

PETER   There isn't anybody out there   *(Long knock)*   *(KNOCK.)*

OSCAR. I'll take your word for it

PETER. The point is—whether you've decided

LEHMAN   Who's out there?

PETER   It's not anybody. Maybe a book agent. Do you want the show or don't you?

LEHMAN   Now look here, Sweetheart, that's a big bundle of coin   You can't expect us—— *(A more insistent knock)*   Oh, for Heaven's sake! Why don't you send him away?   *(KNOCK)*

PETER   Don't worry about him   *(Gets idea)*   I

can't send him away—anyway—I can't send him
away—till you've decided

LEHMAN What?

PETER Do you want to know who it is? I'll tell
you——

LEHMAN. I don't care as long as he stops his
racket.

PETER All right I'll tell you who it is—if you
really want to know That's a fellow who wants
to take over most of the show—that's who that is
*(Pause MAC turns quickly to R and LEHMAN looks
at him.)*

OSCAR Is it?

PETER Yes, sirree. You'd be surprised if you
knew who that was   *(KNOCK.)*

LEHMAN *(Knock)* Who is it?

PETER He's a man that does things just like that
(Snaps fingers) and if you don't want it, all right
I'll open the door right up, and——

LEHMAN Wait a minute Mac! Hurry up

PETER If you want it you'd better give me your
checks before he comes in, or——

LEHMAN. Hurry up, Mac! *(Hands PETER check)*
Here! Now it's ours. *(Business with money and receipt.)*

OSCAR What's going on here?

PETER. *(Gets checks)* That's all right They've
just bought the show back again   ∕

OSCAR I—I get my money back?

PETER I should say you do They've just paid a
hundred thousand dollars for thirty-three and a third
per centum—— *(Crosses to door on laugh)*

LEHMAN For what?

PETER *(Unlocks and opens door R)* This gentleman will tell you all about it Oh, Mr Patterson—
(PATTERSON enters R) This gentleman is Mr Patterson—Mr. A J Patterson—a lawyer at law, and

he wants sixty-six and two-thirds percent on account of that short story. Remember?

LEHMAN   Oh, he does, eh?

PETER.   Mr. Lehman has just bought the show back again, Mr Patterson. *(Crosses to* JANE *at desk; gives her checks, which she keeps)*

PATTERSON   Indeed?

OSCAR. *(Takes up* C *)* Yes, indeed.

LEHMAN. *(Crosses to* PATTERSON*)* Yah, and I know all about that phoney case   You ain't got no more grounds than a rabbit.

PATTERSON   We have a perfect case.

LEHMAN.   Yah?   Well, there's one thing you don't know. *(Looks at others)* There ain't been a hit produced in twenty years that——*(Leads* PATTERSON *off* R *)* some guy ain't said it was swiped from him *(Both exit* R *; shuts door.)*

MAC   *(Crosses* R *)* You certainly disappointed me. *(Exits* R *, closing door)*

LEHMAN   *(Voice off* R *)* Last year in London——

OSCAR   Gee, this is great! You mean it—I get my money back?

PETER   You get forty-nine thousand dollars

OSCAR.   This is going to be an awful lesson to me

LEHMAN. *(Voice off stage)* And there's another thing you don't know——

OSCAR. *(Crosses to door* R. *and opens)* I want to hear what he's saying

LEHMAN   *(Off* R *)* Ten years ago from a guy named Sheridan—— (OSCAR *exits   Closes door* R   PETER *at door* R *, listens)*

FANNY   And I came here to look after you two. *(Crosses to* D *to* C *)*

JANE   *(Rises, crosses to* FANNY'S L *)* We couldn't have done it without you   And we do appreciate it——enormously.

PETER   *(At* FANNY'S R.*)* I should say we do   I'll never forget it. I'll never forget the *whole* thing.

And if Mr Lehman does anything to you, just you let me know.

FANNY   *(Nods head)*   I'll get along all right *(*OSCAR *enters* R *)*

LEHMAN.   *(Off* R *)*   And you're getting a bargain, too

OSCAR.   *(Closes door* R *)*   I just came in to tell you the good news.

PETER   What?

OSCAR.   Mr. Lehman is going to let me buy my share *back* again.   (PETER *crosses up and leans on file cabinet*   FANNY, C *, looks at* JANE, L C *)*

FANNY   Let me out first   *(Crosses* R *)*   Oh, well —good-bye

PETER   *(Crosses to* C *)*   Good-bye

FANNY   At that maybe you're not such a sucker You certainly put it over   But how that charade ever turned out to be a hit is a mystery to your Aunt Sadie   *(Opens door* R *and exits, closing door*)

OSCAR   Could you let me have my share of the money right away—to give Mr Lehman?

PETER   Now—now look here, Oscar——

OSCAR.   But I'm afraid Mr Lehman won't wait

PETER   He'll wait, but——   Gosh!   You don't want to go back into the theatrical business   *(To* JANE*)*   Does he?

(WARN Curtain)

JANE   Of course not.

OSCAR.   Don't I?

PETER   You know where you ought to be—a man like you?   In the hotel business   Shouldn't he?

JANE   Of course

OSCAR   But last time you said I ought to get out of it.

PETER   Oh, that was different   Listen, have you ever been in Chillicothe?

OSCAR   No

PETER. Well, it's a wonderful place—there's a wonderful town, Oscar. Jane and I are going there. Aren't we, Jane? *(Crosses to* JANE *)*

JANE. I hope so

PETER. *(Crosses back to* OSCAR*)* You bet we are! We're going back to Chillicothe, and buy a hotel, see—for fifty thousand dollars—and with your money too it could be made one of the greatest hotels in the world—anywhere.

OSCAR But now—now, wait——

JANE It's a real chance, Mr. Fritchie. The chance of a lifetime.

PETER It'll be wonderful, see? We'll build a great big addition—— It'll be the greatest hotel that —I'll sell you forty-nine per cent of it for—here— sit down, Sweetheart—— *(As* FRITCHIE *sits in chair* R *of desk Ring curtain.)* Now, look This is going to be one of the—— *(Ad lib as Curtain falls.)*

CURTAIN

"THE BUTTER AND EGG MAN"

PROPERTY PLOT

ACT I

Bundles of newspapers.
Bespangled costume.
Ballet-dancer's slipper.
Photographs on wall.
Cigars (Lehman).
Cigarettes (Mac).
On desk:
       'Phone
       Ashtray.
       Papers, stationery, writing material.
       Receipt book.
In desk:
       Cigar box.
       Route sheet.
Check (Martin).
Checkbook (Peter).

ACT II

Box of roses (in closet).
WAITER:
       Tray.
       Wine glasses.
       Knives, forks, plates, napkins.
       Service table.
       Trays of food and sandwiches.
       2 bottles of wine in coolers
       Meal check.

Notebook, manuscript, pencil (Jane).
Chairs (off L.)
Money (Peter).
Gigars (Lehman).
Checkbook (Oscar).
Paper of notes (Peter).

ACT III

Brief case containing documents ˙nd magazine
    (Patterson).
Newspapers (on desk).
PETER:
    Cane.
    Cigarette case.
    Cigarettes.
    Holder.
Card (Jane).
Checks (Lehman and Mac).

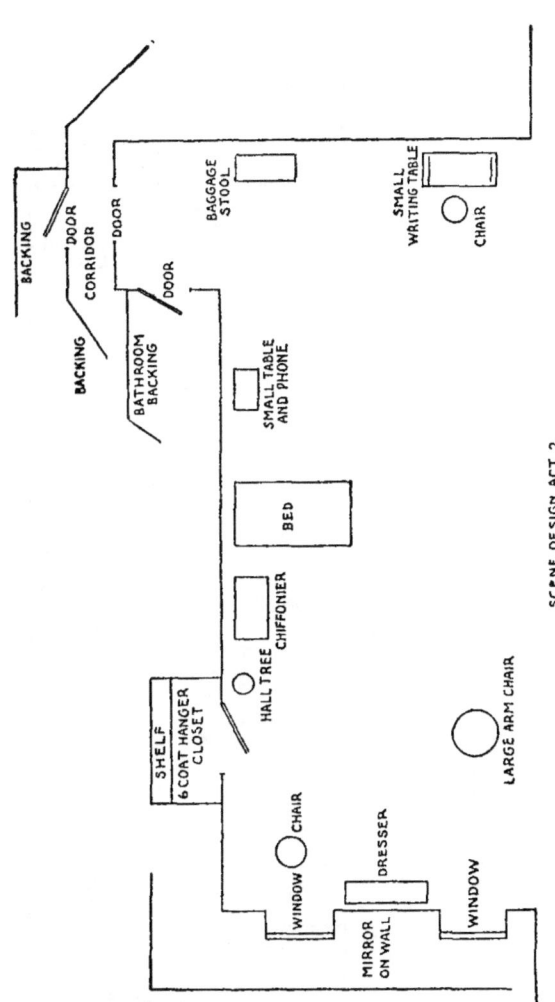

SCENE DESIGN ACT 2
"THE BUTTER AND EGG MAN"

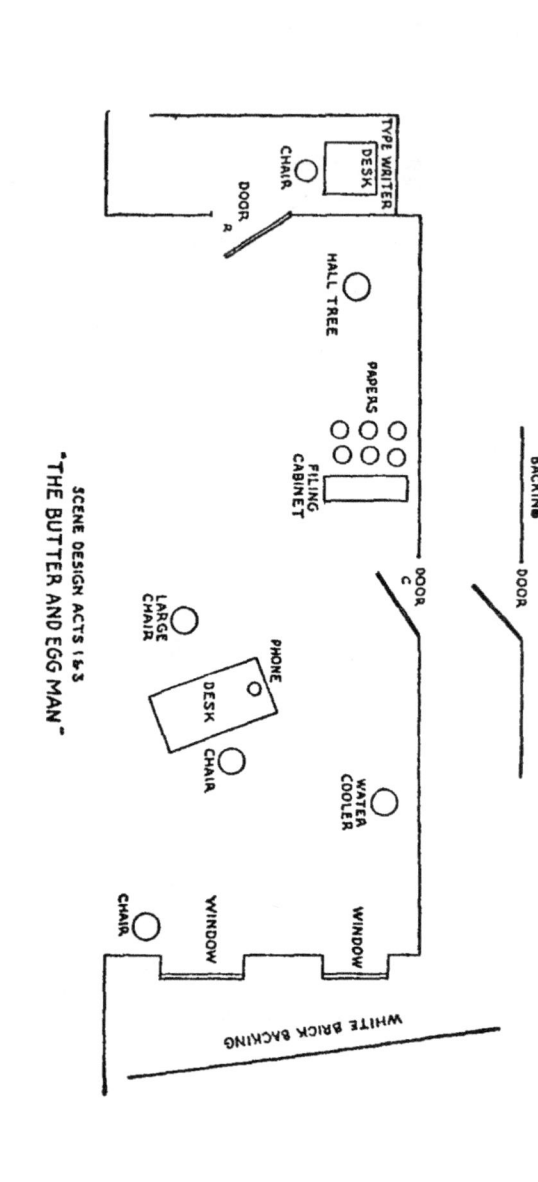

SCENE DESIGN ACTS 1 & 3
"THE BUTTER AND EGG MAN"

www.ingramcontent.com/pod-product-compliance
Lightning Source LLC
Chambersburg PA
CBHW070342120726
47909CB00008B/2718